ALIEN INVASION!

GUY BASS

ILLUSTRATED BY FRED BLUNT

■SCHOLASTIC

TO RUTH, FOR BELIEVING IN ALIENS!

First published in the UK in 2010 by Scholastic Children's Books
An imprint of Scholastic Ltd
Euston House, 24 Eversholt Street
London, NW1 1DB, UK
Registered office: Westfield Road, Southam, Warwickshire, CV47 0RA
SCHOLASTIC and associated logos are trademarks and/or registered trademarks
of Scholastic Inc.

ISBN 978 1 407 11120 9

A CIP catalogue record for this book is available
from the British Library.

Printed by CPI, Bookmarque, Croydon, CR0 4TD
Papers used by Scholastic Children's Books are made from
wood grown in sustainable forests.

1 3 5 7 9 10 8 6 4 2

www.scholastic.co.uk/zone

LEND A SUCKER:
YOUR PLANET NEEDS
YOU!

AVOID DISINTEGRATION – JOIN THE
INVASION EFFORT!

HEY!
HEY YOU, THERE! YES, YOU WITH THE ANTENNA!

THINKING OF BEING A SPACE INVADER?

STOP!

YOU NEED THE ALL-NEW
PLANET X PERSONAL ADVICE DEVICE
(VERSION 2.0.2.5.8.1.7.7.4.2.2)

*The **Planet X PERSONAL ADVICE DEVICE** (or **P.A.D.**) tells you*
everything you ever needed to know
Simply ask it a question and your P.A.D. will search its
12,000,000,0000,000,000,000,000 gigafrooms of data to keep you
up-to-date and on your way to being the best space invader
ever to pilot a hypersaucer!

No question too tricky! No topic is too obscure!
*Never fear – the **P.A.D.** is here!*

The P.A.D. – giving you everything you wanted to know about space invading, but were afraid to ask.

A NICE DAY FOR
SPACE INVADING

It was sixteen o'clock on the third Valoonaday in the month of Green, and Hex (or Hex-37 to give him his full name) was huddled under his duvet, tinkering away at his latest robot creation.

"Primary control module looking good . . . limbs responsive – let's see if he ticks," Hex said. He flicked a small switch and then closed the control panel on the back of the robot's head. As he held it in one of his suckers, the small, round robot hummed and buzzed into life – blinking with confusion.

"Well, hello there," said Hex.

"Chik-POP!" said the little robot.

"Sorry, I still haven't worked out how to make you talk properly," said Hex, as the robot spun its tiny arms around. "But don't worry, I've always spoken pretty good 'robot'."

"Chik-POP!" said the robot, happily.

"That's just what I was going to say! You know, I think you might be my best robot yet," said Hex, proudly. "I'm going to call you Glitch. My name is He-EEEEEYOW!"

A long metal pincer grabbed Hex by the ankle, lifting him out of his slumber pod.

"YOoOW! Knock it off T.K., I'm awake, I'm awake!" screeched Hex.

"Another beautiful day on Planet X! The suns are shining, the air is very nearly non-toxic, and there's only a 32.4 per cent chance of meteor showers!" said T.K.421, the computer that ran Hex's fully automated floating home high in the skies of Planet X.

The pincer dropped Hex on to the floor

and then snaked back into the wall. Hex picked up his little robot and checked that it wasn't broken.

"Are you OK, Glitch?"

"POP-glik!" said Glitch, his head spinning around.

"Why, you've made a little robot! How clever," said T.K. "Not as clever as me, of course, but then I am a T.K.4 model – the cleverest home computers since the T.K.3! No other home computer is more dedicated to making a comfortable environment for the modern space invader! So what does your little robot do? Shoot death rays? Launch mutation spores?"

"He doesn't do anything. I just made him for fun," said Hex. There was a pause. Finally, T.K. replied, "Does not compute – 'fun' is not a function."

"It's not supposed to. . . I'll explain later," Hex sighed. "I'd better get ready for school."

"Absolutely! It's your first day at Sporg's School for Space Invaders!" said T.K.421, excitedly. "Oh, Master Hex, your father would be *so* proud to see you start your training! If he wasn't lost somewhere in deep space, that is."

"Thanks for reminding me, T.K.," Hex grumbled. He stretched his antenna, and stepped lazily on to the conveyor-floor. "Cleansing zone, please."

"Faster than a hypersaucer hopping to light speed, Master Hex!" said T.K. and the conveyor-floor whisked Hex out of his room, down the hall and into the cleansing zone so fast that he could barely stay on his feet. As a cleansing tube lowered around him, Hex looked at his image in the reflector. Apart from looking tired (his telepathy nodes were *particularly* swollen), Hex was bright green with two large, round eyes and a bulbous head. Out of the top of his head grew a long, single antenna. He rubbed his eyes with his suckers and yawned out of his gills.

"Just give me the basic rinse," he mumbled, as T.K.'s cleansing programme whirred into action.

SKOOSH! CHUNG! ZWORT! VWASH! SKWETCH!

"YoOOooOOW! Oo! *Ow!* Uff! GAH!" cried Hex, as the cleansing tube sprayed, rubbed and scrubbed.

"You can't very well start space invader school without polished eyeballs and scrubbed suckers, now can you?" said T.K. eagerly as Hex was conveyed into the clothing zone. "Arms up!" said T.K. as more robotic pincers shot out of the wall, holding various items of clothing.

Two point nine seconds later, Hex was dressed. He was wearing a shiny, silvery uniform, large magna-boots and a brand new tele-belt. Hex made sure the belt was set to OFF (he didn't want it accidentally picking up a teleportation signal and transporting him who knows where) and then slipped Glitch into his pocket just as he was delivered into the ingestion zone.

"You're 3.5 seconds late for breakfast, Hex-37," said Hex's mother as she swept into the ingestion zone. She straightened his antenna as she passed by and sat down. The light of the planetexian suns shone through the window into her huge, translucent brain-sack, illuminating her pulsating brain. "You know what they say," she continued, "laziness leads to lateness, lateness leads to disintegration."

"Yes, Mum," sighed Hex, as a bowl of grey gloop was plonked on to the table in front of him. He stared at it and scrunched up his face. "Gloop again for breakfast, then?"

"You know what they say – a bowl of gloop a day keeps the medical droid away," said his mother. Gloop was the only food on Planet X. All other foods had been "gloopified" to become an ingredient in gloop. Gloop tasted sort of like everything, which meant it sort of tasted like nothing, and Hex hated it.

"Scoop that gloop! It's got everything a space invader needs!" said T.K., as a spoon arm extended from the wall and slopped more gloop into Hex's bowl.

"Today is a big day for you, Hex," said his mother. "You could work hard at your training and be a great space invader, like me. Or you could be lazy and end up lost in space, like your father."

Hex sighed. His mother always insisted that Hex's dad was just lazy, as he had never managed to graduate from space invader school. But Hex knew different. He knew that his dad was the victim of a terrible family curse – the "Hex Effect". The Hex Effect followed one general rule: once any male Hex started space invading training, everything went horribly, horribly wrong. There was nothing they could do about it. Hex's dad had it, as did his dad before him, and so on, for thirty-six generations. In fact, the Hexes were the only planetexians in history never to have done any actual invading:

✡ **Hex-36 – Sucked into a black hole**

during hypersaucer training

✡ **Hex-35 – Teleported into deep space during tele-belt training**

✡ **Hex-34 – Permanently transmogrified into a six-bellied skweech during mutation ray class**

✡ **Hex-33 – Disintegrated on the toilet (no one really knows how)**

Not surprisingly, Hex was more than a bit concerned about starting space invader school. In fact, he could think of nothing worse. Unfortunately, on Planet X, space invading was all anyone ever seemed to care about.

"Do I *really* have to go?" asked Hex, failing to notice Glitch climb out of his pocket and clamber down the chair to the floor.

"Of course you have to go! How are you going to learn to be a space invader otherwise?" said his mother, as if the suggestion was completely ridiculous. She paused for a moment, and then rested her suckers on Hex's shoulders. "Listen to me, Hex. You're a very talented boy. There isn't a piece of technology on Planet X that you couldn't take apart and put back together. But you have a *duty* to put your talents to space invading, not wasting them making silly little robots. I mean, if only they had *something* to do with invading . . . you could have built a sentry-bot, like the ones that guard the empress. At least they have ray-guns."

"They're not *supposed* to have anything to do with space invading," said Hex, grumpily. "They're just robots."

"Then there's no point in making them, is there?" continued his mother. "I mean it this time, Hex. It's time that you focus on the important things in life – space and invading. Do I make myself clear?" She began striding around the kitchen, as Glitch zoomed between her legs. "Look around you. Everything we have we got as a result of space invading. Space invading is what we do – it's *all* we do! Planetexians didn't get where we are building useless little toys which do nothing except get underfoot!"

KRUNCH!

Hex looked down. His mother had stepped on Glitch!

"My robot! Glitch, are you OK?" shouted Hex, jumping down from the table and scooping Glitch up. "Talk to me! How many suckers am I holding up?" he added, but Glitch's head fell off and clunked to the floor.

"You see? This is *exactly* what I'm talking about," said his mother. "How do you expect to be a space invader if you're not thinking about space invading?"

"Space invading is stupid!" growled Hex, angrily, as he picked up Glitch's head. "I don't even want to be a space—"

"*Shhhhhh!*" said his mother, slapping a sucker over his mouth. "Do you want to be disintegrated? You know better than to question the will of the empress! Honestly, Hex, what would your father say if he heard you talking like that?"

"Given that he's lost in outer space, I'd be pretty surprised if he can hear me!" said

Hex, putting Glitch's crumpled parts back into his pocket.

"Yes, well, perhaps if he'd taken his space invader training seriously, he wouldn't have messed everything up so badly," said his mother. She shook her head and turned on the morning news-vid.

"The wait is almost over! After months of voting, the final four contenders for invasion have been selected, and tonight, live from the palace, Her Majestic Green, the Empress Valoona XIII, will decide which planet will next be conquered by the planetexian invasion force. The empress, in her infinite and unquestioned wisdom, will make the selection using the traditional method of sticking a pin in a map whilst blindfolded.

"The shortlist for the soon-to-be-renamed PLANET X number 914 (or thereabouts) are:

> *PLANET ZAXON (odds of 6:1)*
> *PLANET STELA (odds of 5:1)*
> *PLANET INSTA (odds of 20:1)*
> *PLANET EARTH (odds of 100:1)*

The decision will be announced this afternoon, at twenty o'clock. Invaders! Place your bets and charge your ray-guns!"

*

"Wonderful news!" said his mother. "Just think, Hex, if you do well in your training, you might even get fast-tracked to the invasion fleet!"

"Invasion day always comes around so fast," sighed Hex. "I thought we'd just got settled here – on *this* Planet X."

"You know what they say – those who can, invade. Those who can't, get disintegrated," said his mother, her huge, oval eyes glazing over as she recalled her days as a captain of the 101st hypersaucer fleet. She couldn't wait to invade the next planet!

"Only five minutes until the skybus arrives! Time to go!" cried T.K. loudly, shooting a pincer out of the wall and plucking Hex from his seat.

"I'm ready, I'm ready!" said Hex as T.K. dropped him on to the conveyor. His mother rested her sucker on the top of his head.

"I know you'll make me proud, Hex," she said. A moment later she added, "You will, won't you?"

Hex didn't reply. He just waited until he was whisked into the ejection chute and fired on to the waiting platform. He could already see the snake-like skybus stopping at each of the floating homes. He took a deep breath and stared at the two bright suns in the pink planetexian sky as the skybus pulled up at the docking platform.

"All aboard!" said the driver. Hex looked back, to see his mother (and one of T.K.'s robotic hands) waving at him through the window. He weakly waved a sucker, and then got on.

SPORG'S SCHOOL FOR SPACE INVADERS

"Next stop, Sporg's School for Space Invaders," said the skybus driver, and a cheer went up from each of the 118 excited planetexian children. In fact, everyone cheered except Hex. He slinked down the skybus looking for a spare seat.

As he shuffled down the aisle, the other children pressed their faces against the windows as the skybus passed over the emerald palace of Empress Valoona. The palace seemed to shimmer in the morning light, and Hex imagined the empress inside – plotting the invasion of planet after planet. Hex could hardly believe that a matter of years ago, this whole world had been pretty much flattened by the invading planetexian army. No one was allowed to talk about what it used to be called or who used to live here, but everyone seemed to have forgotten anyway. All that mattered was that it had been rebuilt and renamed as *the new* Planet X.

"You can sit next to me if you like!" said a voice. It came from the biggest boy Hex had ever seen. He was a brighter green than Hex, with a huge round belly and head, and stubby little legs. He smiled and eagerly patted the seat next to him.

"Uh, thanks," said Hex, trying to squeeze on to what little seat there was left.

"We're going to be space invasers!" said the giant boy, excitedly. "Can you believe it?"

"Uh, I suppose," said Hex, a little nervous.

"I can't believe they make us wait so long before we start! I've been wanting to blow stuff up since I was an egg!" the boy said, making a ray-gun shape with his suckers. "BOOM! BOOM!"

"M-me too," said Hex, checking to see if there were any other free seats around.

"Great! We can be invasing buddies! I'm Dooper. What's your name?" asked the boy.

"Hex," mumbled Hex.

"Team Dooper and Hex. . ." Dooper mused. "Sounds good! 'Look at Team Dooper and Hex go!' they'll say. 'Did you see that? Team Dooper and Hex invased that whole planet with one sucker tied behind their backs! BOOM! Here's a medal and some extra gloop for Team Dooper and Hex! The best space invasers on Planet X!' That's what they'll say!"

"Yeah, that's what they'll say," said Hex, forcing a smile.

"Actually," said another voice behind him, "I think you'll find that the title of best space invader on Planet X will be going to *me*."

Hex turned around to see a pointy-faced boy stared at him with narrow, black eyes. He was wearing a 3D holo-badge that read INVADER-IN-TRAINING.

"My name is Steek," he said, as if everyone should already know who he was. Hex and Dooper just looked back blankly. "My father was Steek-55, captain of the 229th hypersaucer fleet, which led the invasion of this Planet X. He said I have what it takes to be the best of the best!"

"Better than Team Dooper and Hex?" said Dooper. "No way! We're going to invase everywhere – twice! Isn't that right, Hex?"

"Uh. . ." began Hex.

"Wait a minute . . . *Hex*? You're Hex? Not Hex-37? 'Hex Effect' Hex?" said Steek, examining him with disdain.

"Do I know you?" asked Hex, wondering how on Planet X this boy knew about the Hex Effect.

"I know *you* – you're Hex-37! Your dad was Hex-36," snarled the boy. "My dad told me to look out for you! He went to Sporg's with your dad. He said that your dad couldn't even go *near* a hypersaucer or a ray-gun without something going wrong. He said you Hexes are bad luck."

"Um. . . Well. . ." Hex began anxiously, wishing he was the one that was lost in space right now.

"And your dad never even graduated, did he? He was stuck at Sporg's for, like, twenty years?"

Hex took a deep, defeated breath and said, "Twenty two."

"Twenty two? Twenty two years training and he still didn't graduate! By the empress's underpants, he must have been the worst pupil ever!" laughed Steek, but then he fixed Hex with a stern glare. "You'd better stay out of my antenna-range, Hex-37. I'm going to be the greatest space invader in the history of Planet X and the last thing I need is you messing everything up. Understand?"

"I'll be careful," said Hex.

"You'll be dead," said Steek, poking Hex with a sucker.

"Why don't you pick on someone your own size, Stink?" said Dooper.

"It's *Steek*," said Steek, squaring up to Dooper. "And I'd have to eat all the gloop on Planet X to be *your* size. Even your antenna is fat!"

"I am not fat! I have overactive elbow-glands!" said Dooper, shaking his elbows in Steek's face.

"You're so fat it'd take a hundred hypersaucers just to drag you off that seat!" laughed Steek.

"Oh, put a sock in your gills, Steek," said another voice. Hex turned around to see a girl lean over Steek's chair and grab him by the antenna.

"Ow! Get off, Opo!" yelped Steek. "That hurts!"

"Don't listen to my brother, he's just nervous because Dad isn't here to hold his sucker," said Opo.

"I am not! Shut up, Opo!" whined Steek as he sat back in his seat.

"He's your brother?" asked Hex.

"We're twins. He got all the meanness, I got everything else," said Opo with a grin. "Don't worry, he's all talk. And I'm sure you'll be great invaders," she said, and smiled. Hex blushed a deep shade of green and looked out of the window. He hadn't noticed that the skybus had been descending into the city. They had arrived at Sporg's.

"Last stop, everyone off!" said the skybus driver as they landed outside a huge silvery-white building, with dozens of tall, thin spires ending in vast, spherical learning pods. Hex had never been this far into the city before. As he climbed off the skybus, he was struck with how bright and noisy it was. Everywhere he looked, massive floating billboards bellowed their slogans into the air:

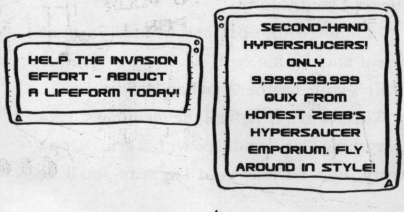

HELP THE INVASION EFFORT - ABDUCT A LIFEFORM TODAY!

SECOND-HAND HYPERSAUCERS! ONLY 9,999,999,999 QUIX FROM HONEST ZEEB'S HYPERSAUCER EMPORIUM. FLY AROUND IN STYLE!

Hex didn't have time to stop and stare – the ever-growing sea of children had begun bundling into the school as skybus after skybus dropped off yet more space invaders in training. Hex was dragged along with the crowd, guided by a horde of spindly assisto-bots into the main hall.

"Move along, no dawdling, tuck in those suckers, there's room enough for everyone," said the assisto-bots, shuffling between the crowd on their thin metal legs. After a while, Hex spotted a fat, imposing-looking old planetexian emerging from the end of the hall on a floating podium.

"File in, file in! That's it!" bellowed the fat planetexian. "I am Sporg-109, but you will call me Headmaster Sporg! Never 'Sporgy'! Only my mother called me Sporgy and I had her disintegrated years ago!"

Dooper yelled, "BOOM!" at the mere mention of disintegration.

"Silence! There shall be no booming in my school unless I say so!" shouted Headmaster Sporg. "As long as there has been space invading, there have been space invader schools! And Sporg's is the best space invader school this side of the space invader school just down the road! Am I right?"

"Yes, Headmaster!" said the assisto-bots.

"Yes, Headmaster!" came the pupils' cry.

"Yes, Headmaster!" yelled Dooper a moment later.

"For those of you returning to Sporg's to continue your five-year training, welcome back!" said Sporg. "I am sure you are all delighted to be back, so that you, too, may become space invaders! After all, what else are you going to do?"

There was confused murmuring from the pupils, as if they had never even thought about doing anything else. Only Hex had a better idea – he took Glitch out of his pocket and set about repairing him.

"Poor Glitch," whispered Hex, trying to reattach Glitch's head. "Don't worry, I'll fix you properly when we get home. . ."

"Shut your gills, Hex, I'm trying to listen!" said Steek. "You might not give a quark about space invading, but I do!"

"SILENCE!" boomed Headmaster Sporg. "Talking, whispering, mumbling and unwarranted telepathy are punishable by disintegration! Now, where was I – oh yes! Those of you who are new to the school, pin back your hear lobes! Here at Sporg's, over the next five years, you will learn all the skills that you need to be a galaxy-class space invader! But for those of you who think that space invading is all about shooting death rays at stuff, you must think again! Oh dear me no – there are hundreds of different ways to take over a planet and you are going to learn them all. You will learn how to pilot a hypersaucer through meteor showers and black holes! You will learn how to carry out abductions and the proper procedures for probing! You will master mind-control, and become masters of disguise! But most importantly, you will learn how to shoot death rays at stuff! Not straight away, of course. There are a good four and a half years of dull theory tests and dreary essays before we get to the good stuff. This is a school, after all! Now, repeat the school motto: *If in doubt, disintegrate!*"

"If in doubt, disintegrate!" repeated the assisto-bots together.

"If in doubt, disintegrate!" shouted the thousands of children. This time Hex did join in, but only because he could see Opo looking at him.

"Remember that motto, and you will never fail. Which is important, because if you *do* fail, you'll be disintegrated," said Headmaster

Sporg. "Now, set your belts to 'receive' and stand by to be teleported to your designated learning pod."

Hex and the other children grabbed the dials on their tele-belts and turned them to receive the teleported beam. A second later, they were bathed in a bright blue light, which transported them instantly from the hall to their learning pods.

Everyone except Hex.

The teleport hadn't worked! Hex looked up at Sporg, who was staring suspiciously at him from the other end of the hall. He frantically turned the dial on his tele-belt as the headmaster floated towards him.

"What's this? Not teleported? Causing trouble already, boy? And in your first . . ." the headmaster checked his watch and tutted – "2.4 minutes at school, oh dear me no. Didn't you check your tele-belt before you left?"

"No; I mean, yes! Sorry, I don't know what's, I mean, it's not. . ." Hex began, desperately turning the dial until it began to smoke. Finally, the dial popped off in his suckers, and Hex shrieked as the belt exploded!

"Yow!" screamed Hex, and as he unclipped his belt and threw it to the floor, one thought burned in his brain-sack.

The Hex Effect had begun.

THE P.A.D.

"Exploded, eh? The first sign of a poorly maintained tele-belt," said Headmaster Sporg, staring at Hex with all three of his eyes.

"No, but . . . it's brand new! My T.K. unit only took it out of the box this morning," said Hex, gathering up the pieces of his ruined tele-belt. He couldn't believe that the Hex Effect had started already!

"SILENCE!" boomed Headmaster Sporg.

"There are no excuses for excuses," tutted an assisto-bot.

"Under normal circumstances I'd just disintegrate you and be done with it," continued Headmaster Sporg, his brain-sack pulsating. Hex whimpered with fear. "But it is your first day and finding your way to your learning pod on foot might just be punishment enough. There are six hundred and nineteen of them, after all."

"Six hundred and nineteen?" gasped Hex, his wide eyes wider than ever.

"Well, don't just stand there, boy. . ." said the headmaster, his antenna glowing green with rage. "MOVE!!"

Three hours and four minutes of wandering identical-looking corridors later, Hex stumbled across his learning pod, by which time he was wondering why he hadn't just gone home.

"Roswell class," he said, reading the holo-sign on the portal door. Cautiously, he pressed the OPEN button.

"Ah, Hex-37, I assume? How good of you to join us," said the teacher as the portal slid open. "Well don't just stand there like a wingless nudlork, come in, come in." She was a spindly, long-headed planetexian, with a holo-badge that said "Miss Voob".

"Sorry I'm late, I—" began Hex, but Miss Voob just waved him to his desk. He made his way past Dooper, who gave him a suckers-up signal, and Opo, who smiled at him just long enough to make him blush again.

"Not to worry, there's no rush – we're not invading yet!" chuckled Miss Voob. "But what's this? Where's your tele-belt?" continued Miss Voob, pointing at Hex's still smouldering trousers.

"Umm . . . I had a little trouble," said Hex, brushing off the last remnants of the belt from his trousers.

"Well, you must learn to walk before you can teleport, as they say," said Miss Voob. "Then again, we can't have you wandering around the school on foot – you'll wear out your magna-boots! I'm sure there's a spare tele-belt in the lost property box."

Hex waited awkwardly as a large, dusty crate materialized on Miss Voob's desk. She dug both suckers in and fished around, finally pulling out an enormous, ancient tele-belt with both hands. It looked like it belonged in a museum and as Miss Voob handed it to Hex, the class began to snigger.

"Here we are. It looks to be a good few years older than you are, but not to worry. Not sure what happened to the previous owner . . . disintegration, I presume. Still, it'll do for now!" said Miss Voob.

As Hex fixed the massive, outdated tele-belt to his trousers, he felt the whole class stare at him and remembered exactly why he hadn't wanted to come to space invader school in the first place.

"Hey, Hex-37! Why are you wearing your grandma's belt?" shouted Steek, and the class burst into laughter.

"I'd be careful with that," said Opo as Hex settled in his seat. "Those old tele-belts have a habit of sending you wherever they please – you could re-materialize anywhere on Planet X! And who knows how long it'd take to pick up the school's teleporter signal after that."

"Great, thanks for the tip," muttered Hex, nervously. At least he might have a chance to try and repair it when he got home. He'd never taken a tele-belt apart before, but he had a fairly good idea of how it worked.

"Settle down, class!" said Miss Voob. "The time has come for you to receive the most important piece of equipment you will ever need in your invader training. Children, I present to you . . . your P.A.D.s."

Hex watched a small, silver object materialize on his desk. It fitted perfectly into his palm, and had a small screen on the front and a single green button. Hex had seen P.A.D.s before – every grown-up planetexian had one – but he'd never actually used one. Despite himself, he got rather excited about the prospect of having one.

"Look after your Personal Advice Device! This nifty little device will serve as your guide and companion in the days, months and years that follow," said Miss Voob. "Just ask it a question and it will tell you everything you need to know. Now, let's get started! Press the green button to imprint the P.A.D. with your greenetic code. Once you've turned it on, follow the instructions on the screen."

Hex reached out an excited sucker and pressed the button. The P.A.D. played a little jingle and then lit up.

WELCOME TO YOUR PERSONAL ADVICE DEVICE SET-UP WIZARD. THIS WIZARD WILL GUIDE

YOU THROUGH HOW TO PREPARE YOUR P.A.D.
FOR USE. DEPENDING ON THE SPEED OF
YOUR CONNECTION, THE WIZARD MAY TAKE A
FEW MINUTES TO COMPLETE.
YOUR PROGRESS THROUGH THE SET-UP WIZARD
WILL BE SHOWN ON THE DISINTEGRATING
PLANETEXIAN BAR ON THE LEFT. ONCE THE
PLANETEXIAN IS FULLY DISINTEGRATED,
YOUR P.A.D. IS READY TO USE!

CLICK OK TO CONTINUE.

It all seemed fairly simple. Hex reached out
a sucker and clicked OK.

134;P 92E8F# 3RY 9P3##4981U3O4T 813!!
RECEIVING/DECODING...PLEASEWAIT...

Hex waited. Then waited a bit longer. He
looked around. Everyone else already
seemed asking their P.A.D.s questions and
getting answers! Then, finally:

SIGNAL CANNOT BE DECODED.
UNKNOWN ERROR HAS OCCURRED.

PERMANENT FATAL ERROR X.
P.A.D. WILL NOW SHUT DOWN.

Suddenly, the screen went black.

"What? No, wait, come back!" cried Hex, staring at the screen. It could only mean one thing – the Hex Effect had returned!

"Is that Master Hex I can hear, shrieking like a Yoopie? Not having more trouble, are you?" said Miss Voob. Hex's unconvincing "Umm . . . no, Miss Voob", was drowned out by the children all laughing at him.

"Oh dear, oh dear. I do hope you haven't broken your P.A.D.," said Miss Voob. "I don't have any replacements and you know the punishment for destruction of planetexian property."

"DISINTEGRATION!" shouted the children together.

"What? *Really?*" said Hex, wishing he'd paid more attention to all those public service vid-announcements on "How to be a

Good Citizen (And Not Get Disintegrated)".

"But I didn't break it! I just did what it told me! It must be a faulty dynamizing chip – it's not my fault!" protested Hex, but Miss Voob was already striding towards him. He hid the P.A.D. behind his back, pressing the green button over and over. He chewed nervously on a sucker as Miss Voob loomed over him.

"Well?" she said, sternly.

"Yes, I'm quite well, thank you," said Hex, meekly. "How are you?"

"Oh, I'm fine, thanks for – now hang on! I didn't walk all the way over here for a chat! Hex-37, show me your P.A.D. this minute."

"But I didn't, I mean it wasn't, I mean. . ." he said in a very small voice, and brought his P.A.D. from behind his back. As he held it up, he caught sight of Steek, grinning and making a sucker-to-the-head sign (the universal symbol for "You're *so* going to get disintegrated"). Hex screwed his eyes up in horrible anticipation.

"Well, that all seems in order," said Miss Voob. "Don't forget to write your name on the back in permanent marker."

Hex opened an eye and peered at his P.A.D.

```
REBOOT SUCCESSFUL
THE SET-UP IS COMPLETE. YOUR P.A.D.
IS NOW READY TO USE.
HAVE A NICE DAY!
```

"How did. . ." he began, then caught sight of Steek looking disappointed. Hex couldn't help but smile. He may not have escaped the Hex Effect, but it was almost worth it to wipe the smirk off Steek's face.

EVERYTHING YOU WANTED TO KNOW ABOUT SPACE INVADING (BUT WERE AFRAID TO ASK)

"Hey . . . hey, Hex!" shouted Dooper, in his best whisper, as Miss Voob explained the lesson-plan for the entire year. "There's a quiz on my P.A.D.! It says I'm going to be the best space invaser ever!"

"Masters Dooper and Hex! Don't make me disintegrate you!" said Miss Voob. "Unless I'm wasting my gill-breath and you *already know* what you're going to be learning in week thirty nine of your training?"

"Umm. . ." said Dooper, looking around as if the answer might appear in the air. Hex used the distraction to inspect his P.A.D. He whispered the word "Quiz" as quietly as he could, and the P.A.D. pinged into life once more.

IT LOOKS LIKE YOU ARE TRYING TO TAKE A QUIZ. CAN I HELP?

CLICK YES TO CONTINUE.

Hex clicked YES.

WELCOME TO THE PLANET X QUIZ! THIS QUIZ WILL TELL YOU EXACTLY HOW SUITED YOU ARE TO SPACE INVADING AND WHETHER YOU ARE LIKELY TO MAKE IT THROUGH YOUR FIRST INVASION INTACT. NOW LET'S BEGIN:

QUESTION 1. IT IS THE END OF THE DAY AND YOU ARE ALL TUCKED UP IN YOUR SLUMBER POD. YOU NOD OFF, LOOKING FORWARD TO ANOTHER DAY OF SPACE INVASION-RELATED EXCITEMENT. DO YOU DREAM OF:
A) SPACE INVADING
B) SPACE INVASION-RELATED ACTIVITIES, SUCH AS DEATH RAY TARGET PRACTICE
C) BEING DISINTEGRATED
D) NONE OF THE ABOVE

Hex sighed and pressed "d". He often dreamed of far off worlds, but not once had he dreamed of blowing them up with a death ray. What was the point of travelling all that way just to blow something up?

QUESTION 2. ON A SCHOOL TRIP TO THE PLANET X OBSERVATORY, YOU CATCH SIGHT OF A BRAND NEW PLANET. DO YOU:
A) REPORT IT IMMEDIATELY TO PLANET X HIGH COMMAND (OR A TEACHER) SO THAT IT CAN BE ADDED TO THE INVASION LIST
B) TRAIN A LONG-RANGE DEATH RAY ON IT AND BLAST IT FROM A SAFE DISTANCE
C) DO NOTHING, AND RISK DISINTEGRATION
D) NONE OF THE ABOVE

Hex was already starting to see a pattern emerge, and he didn't like where things were heading. He pressed "d" again and moved on.

QUESTION 3. WHEN YOU GROW UP, DO YOU WANT TO BE:

```
A)   A SPACE INVADER
B)   AN INVADER OF SPACE
C)   DISINTEGRATED
D)   NONE OF THE ABOVE
```

Hex shook his head. The quiz wasn't getting him anywhere! He skipped the question and went straight to the results.

```
IF YOU MAINLY ANSWERED A) YOU ARE A
GREAT SPACE INVADER, DEDICATED TO THE
CONQUEST OF ALL PLANETS IN THE NAME
OF HER MAJESTIC GREEN, THE EMPRESS
VALOONA XIII.
IF YOU MAINLY ANSWERED B) YOU HAVE
POTENTIAL, BUT THERE IS STILL WORK
TO BE DONE. REPORT TO YOUR NEAREST
CONDITIONING ZONE FOR EXTRA TRAINING.
IF YOU MAINLY ANSWERED C) YOU WILL BE
DISINTEGRATED.
IF YOU MAINLY ANSWERED D) YOU WILL BE
DISINTEGRATED.

DO YOU WANT TO SAVE YOUR RESULTS?
YES / NO
```

Hex quickly pressed NO. The last thing he needed was another reason to be disintegrated.

"So, how did you do?" said Opo, leaning towards him. "Do you have what it takes to be a space invader?"

"Uh . . . sure! Yeah, straight As all round. I'm all about the invading! There isn't a minute that goes by that I don't think about blowing stuff up!" said Hex, suddenly rather eager to fit in.

"That's right! Team Dooper and Hex!" shouted Dooper.

"That's nothing – look at *this*," said Steek, flashing his P.A.D. in Hex's face. "My P.A.D. just told me I'm going to be the greatest space invader since Zom-2, inventor of the anti-death-ray death-ray!" boasted Steek.

"Really? Did you mention that you still wet your slumber pod?" said Opo.

"I do not! Shut up, Opo!" screeched Steek.

"You lot! *Please* stop dawdling and switch your tele-belts to 'receive'. Didn't you hear the lunch signal?" said Miss Voob, impatiently. "There's only so much gloop in the Big Gloop Bowl to go around."

Hex looked around. He'd been so engrossed in the one-answer-fits-all quiz that he hadn't even noticed the rest of the class had already teleported.

"See you there!" said Dooper, as he set his tele-belt to "receive". Hex took a deep breath, and reluctantly activated his tele-belt, which rumbled and spluttered like a dying gawker-bird. As he began to de-materialize, Hex crossed his suckers. . .

GLOOPED

Hex felt himself re-materialize and nervously opened his eyes. One thing was certain – he wasn't in the ingestion zone. He was inside a large metal cylinder with a hole in the top and a pipe leading upwards. He looked up through the hole, but it was too dark. Where had his belt sent him? Didn't Opo mention something about re-materializing *anywhere* on Planet X? It didn't take long before Hex started to panic.

"Help! Is anyone out there? I'm stuck in a . . . someplace!" he began, but his cries were quickly drowned out by a loud, rumbling sound coming from above him. Hex looked up again.

"*What is that?*" he whispered to himself. A second and a half later, a tidal wave of gloop cascaded on top of him!

"*Gl-mmUm-FFffpH!*" grunted Hex as gloop poured into the cylinder. Hex tried desperately to swim through the flood of foodstuff, but it was hopeless! The gloop kept coming, until the cylinder was full. Hex held his breath as best he could, but gloop filled his gills, his hear-holes, even his belly-nostril! He was about to pass out when, through the sea of gloop, he heard a strange noise.

VWEEEEEEE — CHUNG!

Suddenly, Hex felt himself moving . . . no, falling! The bottom of the cylinder opened up, and the gloop (and Hex) plummeted downwards!

S L O O o o o o o o o o O O O O O R R R R T !

Hex splash-landed into a huge bowl, and the gloop landed on top of him! He scrambled and spluttered his way to the surface of the gloop and grabbed on to the side of the bowl.

"AAAH! Gloop monster!" shrieked Steek, spotting Hex from halfway down a long table.

Hex wiped the gloop from his eyes and looked around. He was in the ingestion zone . . . inside the Big Gloop Bowl! He slowly realized what had happened – his useless, ancient tele-belt had teleported him inside the gloop tube suspended above the bowl and the tube had squeezed him out, along with 500 gallons of grey goo! The bowl rested in the centre of an impossibly long table, with the thousands of pupils sitting around it. Every one of them turned to look at Hex.

"Oh no. . ." Hex mumbled through a mouthful of gloop. The Hex Effect was in full swing and he was only halfway through his first day. To make matters worse, he was

surrounded by a hundred flying ladle-bots that were zooming around the gloop bowl, spooning out the gloop and carrying it to the children.

"Ow! Yowch! Geddof!" said Hex as the ladle-bots banged into him, or tried to scoop him up in their tiny spoon-arms. A wave of laughter began with the children closest to the Big Gloop Bowl, and soon spread through the entire ingestion zone. It was enough to get the attention of Headmaster Sporg.

"What's this? A boy in my gloop? How irregular!" bellowed Headmaster Sporg. "Oh dear me no, this won't do at all! Assisto-bots, bring him to me!"

Hex clambered out of the Big Gloop Bowl as a dozen or so assisto-bots emerged from the far corners of the hall and clanked towards him. Before Hex knew it, the assisto-bots had grabbed him in their pincers. Hex dripped gloop all the way down the long table (splashing a bit on Steek, which was a bonus) as he was dragged to the end and plonked in front of Headmaster Sporg.

"What on Planet X is going on today?" asked Headmaster Sporg, peering at Hex through his third eye. "First I have a pupil with a defective tele-belt, and now this! Is this any way for future space invaders to conduct themselves?"

Hex decided not to mention that he *was* the boy with the defective tele-belt. He was just grateful that the gloop seemed to have disguised his appearance.

"Now, I like a bowl of gloop as much as the next planetexian, but there's no excuse for greediness! A true space invader would never eat more than his share, for he would be taking food from the collective mouth of the planetexian people! The invasion effort must come first!"

"I wasn't trying to eat the—" began Hex.

"Silence! Listening to your argument will take up precious gloop-eating time!" boomed Headmaster Sporg. "No, there's nothing else for it. An example must be made! Now then, what punishment suits the crime? Oooooh, I know! Disintegration!"

"WHAT?" cried Hex. "But . . . but it wasn't my fault! You can't possibly—"

"Silence! I have spoken!" bellowed Headmaster Sporg, getting to his feet and donning his disintegration hat. "As headmaster of Sporg's School for Space Invaders and Class One Disintegration Decree Deliverer, and in the name of Her Majestic Green, the Empress Valoona, I hereby decree that you – um, gloop-covered boy – shall be forthwith taken from this place to the Disintegration Zone, where you shall be placed into the disintegration pod and blasted to atoms!"

"Wait! You can't!" screamed Hex. "I didn't

do anything! Well, apart from the gloop thing, but that wasn't my fault! It's my—"

"Silence! It is too late – nothing can save you now! Assisto-bots, take him away!" yelled Sporg, and the assisto-bots grabbed Hex by his arms once again. Hex couldn't believe his hear-lobes – he hadn't even made it through one day! He would even rather be a space invader than be disintegrated. He was debating whether to try and make a run for it, when:

"ATTENTION CITIZENS OF PLANET X! HER MAJESTIC GREEN, THE EMPRESS VALOONA, IS ABOUT TO ADDRESS HER PEOPLE! CEASE AND DESIST ALL ACTION, INCLUDING INGESTION, INVASION AND DISINTEGRATION!"

The announcement was so loud it shook the walls of the school. The assisto-bots immediately dropped Hex to the floor, and everyone withdrew their feeding tubes from their bowls. A massive holo-screen appeared in the air above them. On the screen was a fat-faced planetexian wearing a large, ornate crown over a particularly transparent brain-sack. She sat on a huge green throne, surrounded by gleaming green statues of herself.

"Citizens of Planet X, it seems like only yesterday that I sent my armies to invade this fair globe, so that we could rebuild and remake it as the new Planet X. But now the time has come to invade once more! The votes have been counted and verified, and the four finalists have been chosen. So without further ado, the result! I love this bit. . ." said Empress Valoona as she hopped off her throne. She was blindfolded and handed a large drawing pin. She was pointed in the vague direction of a huge green map featuring four distinctive planets.

Hex, meanwhile, quickly realized that

everyone had forgotten about him. Even the assisto-bots were too busy watching the holo-screen to pay him any attention. He got slowly to his feet, and caught sight of his reflection in one of the assisto-bot's well-polished chest panels. He was barely recognizable! He edged out of the ingestion zone as quietly as he could, being careful not to arouse suspicion or leave a trail of gloop for anyone to follow. He had just made it to the pupil purification pod when he heard the cry ring out across the loudspeakers.

"THE EMPRESS HAS CHOSEN! THE NEXT PLANET TO BE INVADED WILL BE . . . EARTH!"

A BRIEF HISTORY
OF EARTH

Hex sneaked out of the pupil purification pod. He was making his way back to the ingestion zone when he was met by a sea of excited children coming towards him. He was carried along the corridor, through the hall and out to the landing zone. He had just started to wonder what all the fuss was about when Opo grabbed him by the arm.

"Hex! Where did you go?" she said. "You missed all the excitement!"

"I . . . er, toilet! I had to go to the relief zone. What's happening? Where's everyone going?" asked Hex.

"Home!" said Opo. "Didn't you hear? The Empress picked a planet! We're on holiday for the rest of the day!"

"But. . ." began Hex, not quite believing he'd managed to escape disintegration.

"Oh, and don't worry, no one recognized you under all that gloop. Well, nearly no one," whispered Opo with a smile.

"I . . . I don't know what you mean," began Hex, as he followed Opo, Dooper and Steek on to their skybus.

"You OK, Hex? What happened to you back there?" asked Dooper, sliding into the seat next to Hex and squashing him against the window.

"I'll tell you later," said Hex, scraping dried gloop out of his gills. "Let's just say I *really* need to fix my tele-belt."

"You know what I heard?" said Steek, flicking Hex's hear lobe. "I heard that earthlings don't even have antennae!"

"My dad says they're blue!" said another boy. "Blue and scaly!"

Before long, everyone on the ship had joined in:

"They have no skin!"

"They smell like nudlork vomit!"

"They shoot fire out of their mouths!"

"They eat each other for fun!"

"They're ninety-six per cent pure evil!"

By the time Hex got home, he wasn't sure what to believe about earthlings. Everyone seemed to have their own idea about them. All he did know was that he wanted to be a space invader less than ever.

"Welcome home, Hex – and death to all earthlings!" cried T.K.

"Oh, so you heard," said Hex, dragging his feet through the front portal.

"It's all over the news-vids! Earth! I almost blew a circuit when I heard."

"So, how was your first day?" said Hex's

mother as Hex took off his magna-boots. "Not *too* eventful, I hope."

"Great, just great," sighed Hex, unclipping his P.A.D. and dropping his massive tele-belt on the floor. "This boy on the skybus knew all about Dad, so now everyone thinks I'm bad luck."

"Hex, how many times do I have to tell you, there's no such thing as bad luck," said his mother. "The Hex Effect isn't real. As far as I'm concerned it was made up as a way of getting out of space invading."

"Oh yeah? Well, if there's no Hex Effect, then how do you explain my tele-belt exploding? Or my P.A.D. going crazy the second I turned it on? Or me ending up inside a giant gloop tube? If that's not bad luck then I don't know what is! I mean, I got sentenced to disintegration! On my first day!"

Hex's mother took a deep breath, and

sighed a long sigh. "I'm sure there's a very simple explanation."

"Oh *really*? Great! That explains everything, then. Panic over. I'm just doomed, that's all, nothing to worry about! Maybe I can get sucked into a black hole too! At least I wouldn't have to be a space invader!" growled Hex, his antenna glowing green. After a moment, he sighed a long sigh and added, "Can I be excused? I need to try and fix this tele-belt."

"What about dinner?" asked his mother, a little taken aback.

"No thanks," said Hex, shuddering. "I'm all glooped out for today."

Hex made his way to his zone and laid the tele-belt out on his slumber pod. He was about to get to work repairing it when he remembered that Glitch was still in his pocket. He placed him next to the tele-belt and stared at them both.

"Well, I did *promise* to fix you," he said, setting the tele-belt aside. "And anyway, I'm pretty sure you're the only thing on this whole planet that has nothing to do with space invading."

Hex spent the next three hours putting Glitch back together. He reattached his head, popped out his dents and reconnected his coupling rods. Finally, stifling his yawns, Hex popped open the control panel on the back of Glitch's head and tweaked his primary control module. One by one, Glitch's arms whirled around, his head turned from side to side and he rolled back and forth, as if he was doing a particularly rubbish dance. It was almost bedtime by the time Hex flicked Glitch's ON switch.

"POP-klik-POP!" said Glitch. He spun his head around gleefully and started rolling around Hex's slumber pod.

"You're welcome!" said Hex. A moment

later, his mother poked her head around the portal.

"I brought you a bowl of gloop," said his mother, coming into his zone. "You know what they say – you can't invade on an empty stomach. Did you manage to get your tele-belt fixed?"

"What? Oh yes, good as new!" said Hex, throwing a pillow over Glitch.

"I've ordered you a new one – it should arrive in a couple of days," said his mother, setting the gloop on his bedside table. "Can't have you at a disadvantage if you're going to become a first-rate space invader! Who knows? You might even get to invade Earth!"

"Great," said Hex, adding, "Mum. . . Are earthlings *really* ninety six per cent pure evil?"

"I heard ninety eight," said his mother, kissing him on the head. "Now go to sleep – it's another big day of training tomorrow."

As his mother left, Hex lifted the pillow off Glitch.

"That was close. I don't think Mum would be too happy to see you around."

"POP-chik!" said Glitch, dashing nervously back under the pillow.

"Good idea, stay out of sight," laughed Hex. He climbed into his slumber pod, but his head was too full of thoughts of Planet Earth for him to sleep. He turned on his P.A.D. and said, "Tell me about Earth."

The P.A.D. pinged into life.

IT LOOKS LIKE YOU ARE TRYING TO INVADE PLANET EARTH. CAN I HELP?

"What? No!" began Hex, but the P.A.D. carried on all the same.

YOUR P.A.D. CAN HELP YOU DECIDE WHICH METHOD OF INVASION SUITS YOU BEST:
HYPERSAUCER ATTACK
LONG RANGE DISINTEGRATION RAY

MIND CONTROL SPORES

OR A METHOD OF YOUR CHOOSING. THERE
ARE LOADS OF GREAT WAYS TO TAKE OVER
THAT STINKING MUD BALL KNOWN AS EARTH!
REDUCE IT TO RUBBLE OR DISGUISE YOURSELF
AS AN EARTHLING AND TAKE OVER FROM THE
INSIDE - YOU DECIDE!

"No, I mean, I want to *know* about Earth.
What's it really like?" asked a frustrated
Hex.

PING!

ALL ABOUT EARTH - A BRIEF HISTORY OF A
STINKING MUD BALL.
<u>THE BIRTH OF EARTH</u>
BILLIONS OF YEARS AGO, TWO FAIRLY
RUBBISH PLANETS CALLED ERR AND THH
CRASHED TOGETHER TO MAKE ONE COMPLETELY
USELESS PLANET KNOWN AS EARTH. COMPOSED
OF EIGHTEEN THOUSAND DIFFERENT KINDS OF
MUD, EARTH IS THE DIRTIEST, MUCKIEST,
MUDDIEST WORLD IN EXISTENCE.

Earth sounded like the worst planet in

the universe! Maybe it could do with being invaded – it didn't sound like it could get any worse. Hex skipped ahead to the next chapter.

<u>LIFE ON EARTH</u>
EARTH WAS THE ONLY PLANET IN ITS GALAXY TO CREATE LIFE, BUT IT WAS STILL THE WORST AT DOING IT. GIVEN THAT EARTH WAS MADE ENTIRELY OF MUD, SO ARE ITS HORRIBLY UNIMPRESSIVE LIFE FORMS. KNOWN AS EARTHLINGS, THESE CREATURES SPEND THEIR DAYS WANDERING AROUND IN MUD, WHILE TALKING ABOUT MUD AND EATING MUD (THAT IS, IF THEY ARE NOT EATING EACH OTHER).

A picture of two earthlings appeared on the screen. They were a sort of pinky-brown colour, with two arms and legs and a strange wiry clump of hair on top of their heads. They didn't even have antennae! Hex got nervous just looking at them. Then he noticed a flashing green button appear on screen, which read "Dare you learn more?" He pressed it without thinking.

<u>WATCH OUT, EARTHLINGS ABOUT!</u>
EARTHLINGS ARE A HIGHLY AGGRESSIVE RACE AND HATE EVERYTHING. THEY ARE CONSTANTLY ANGRY AND SPEND ALL DAY HITTING EACH OTHER WITH STICKS. WHEN THEY RUN OUT OF STICKS, THEY RUN EACH OTHER OVER IN WHEELED VEHICLES OR SHOUT UNTIL THEIR HEADS EXPLODE. EARTHLINGS HATE EVERYTHING IN THE UNIVERSE, AND HAVE TWICE DECLARED OPEN WAR ON PLANET X, EVEN THOUGH THEY DID NOT KNOW IT EXISTED.
EARTHLINGS: BETTER OFF DISINTEGRATED. GET THEM BEFORE THEY GET US!
DID THIS ANSWER YOUR QUESTION? YES/NO

Hex had no idea a planet could be so terrible! Why did earthlings hate Planet X (and everything) so much? Was it because they were made of mud? He felt like he had more questions than before. He was about to ask his P.A.D. another question when,
PING-PING-PING-PING-PING-PING-PING-PING!

"No!" said Hex, grabbing the P.A.D. and frantically pressing the green button. "Don't break again!"

> GH25P97Y6235R8TYH5U; 0YⅢW4TQ358
> RECEIVING/DECODING. . . PLEASE WAIT. . .

It was the message from before! Or something very much like it. Hex closed his eyes and crossed his suckers, hoping that it would magically fix itself like before. Then, as if in answer to his prayers, the pinging stopped. He slowly opened one eye. On the P.A.D.'s screen were two words:

> HELLO HEX.

Hex dropped the P.A.D. in shock! How did it know his name?

"T.K., are you messing with my P.A.D.?" he asked.

"Negative!" said T.K. "It is a violation of imperial directive 89,012.2 to interfere with the property of Her Majestic Green, the Empress Valoona XIII. Laws are there to be obeyed."

Hex picked up the P.A.D. and peeked nervously at the screen.

HELLO HEX. . .
ARE YOU OUT THERE?

Hex looked around, suddenly worried that he was being spied on! What if someone had worked out that he was the boy in the gloop? He would be disintegrated for sure! But then again, what if it was some kind of test, some way of proving how much of a space invader he was? After a moment he took a deep gill-breath and said, "Hello?"

There was another **PING!**

CONTACT HAS BEEN MADE. PLEASE WAIT.

The screen went blank. Hex huddled nervously in the corner of his room, staring at the P.A.D., waiting for something to happen, but the P.A.D.'s screen stayed blank.

"What was that all about?" he said.

"Ka-chik-POP!" said Glitch.

Finally, Hex decided that it was probably just the Hex Effect messing everything up again. Maybe this was just how things were going to be from now on – *unpredictable*. Hex wondered how his dad had managed to live with the Hex Effect for so long. *Not that I'll ever get the chance to ask him,* thought Hex with a sigh. He turned off his P.A.D. and put it under his pillow. Then he patted Glitch goodnight and decided it was probably for the best if he forgot all about today. In fact, Hex decided to pretend it had never even happened.

EARTH-MANIA

The next morning, Hex woke up feeling altogether better about things. The problems of the previous day felt like a distant memory, and Hex decided to try to get excited about space invading. Plus Glitch was as good as new, even if his old tele-belt wasn't. Hex whizzed through the cleansing and clothing zones, and then tucked his little robot into his pocket and hopped on to the conveyor.

"Good morning, Hex," said Hex's mother, when Hex appeared in the ingestion zone. "Have you heard the news?"

"What news?" asked Hex. His mother just grinned and turned on the news-vid.

"*Three months?*" asked Hex in amazement. "But that's so soon!"

"When Planet X invades, it doesn't mess around!" yelled T.K.

"But we just got settled here," sighed Hex.

"You know what they say – a planet can't be destroyed in a day," said his mother. "These things take time. Best to start as soon as possible!"

"I suppose," said Hex, heading towards the ejection chute. He stared at the P.A.D. on his belt and looked back. "Mum? Could my P.A.D. know my name?"

"Your *name*? Of course not," laughed his mother. "You should know that's impossible. Why do you ask?"

"No reason," said Hex. A second later he was fired on to the waiting platform. He could already hear Dooper shouting "BOOM!" as the skybus pulled up.

"HEX!" shouted Dooper as Hex clambered aboard. "I saved you a seat! It's another big day for Team Dooper and Hex! BOOM!"

"Thanks Dooper," said Hex with a smile, squeezing on to the seat next to him. Dooper may have been a little strange, but it was nice to have a sort of friend. Especially since all Hex's previous friends had been home-made robots.

"So, did you get your tele-belt fixed?" asked Dooper.

"Uh, I'm working on it," said Hex, and then noticed Dooper was wearing a holo-badge, which read EARTH GOES

BOOM! Hex looked around. *Everyone* was wearing holo-badges, with slogans like GOODBYE EARTH / HELLO PLANET X! and EARTHLINGS: DISINTEGRATE ON SIGHT! And it wasn't just badges – the children were weighed down with Earth-themed gadgets, gizmos and accessories. From Countdown Clocks (Only 2 months, 3 weeks, 6 days, 19 hours and 22 minutes Till Invasion!) to Earthling Detectors (Detects Earthlings From up to 50 Miles Away!), every aspect of the impending invasion was covered.

Where did they get all this stuff? It's only been one day! thought Hex. He suddenly had a funny feeling in his digestion sack, somewhere between jealousy and apprehension. He stared out of the window at the empress's shimmering green palace, and wondered if she ever had doubts about all this space invading.

"What have you got against invading,

anyway?" said Steek, prodding Hex from across the aisle. He was wearing a holo-badge that had EARTH SUCKS MUD! written on it. "You're haven't even got a holo-badge! What's the matter? Do you *like* earthlings or something?"

"What? No! Of course not!" said Hex, defensively. "I just didn't know all this stuff was available."

"You know what I think? I think you wish you were an earthling!" bellowed Steek, loudly enough for everyone to hear. "Earthling! Earthling! Earth – ow!"

Something hit Steek in the head, bouncing off and landing in Hex's lap. He looked down. It was a holo-badge which read BAD LUCK, EARTHLINGS!

"Keep it," said Opo, shoving

Steek back into his chair. "I've got loads."

"Thanks, I think. . ." said Hex, as the skybus landed outside the school.

"Aren't you sick of being saved by a girl, Hex-37?" said Steek, grumpily.

"Aren't you sick of being shown up by your sister?" replied Hex. Steek just huffed and pushed his way off the skybus, and Hex, Dooper and Opo all grinned in unison.

Before long, everyone had filed into the hall where Headmaster Sporg was waiting.

"Welcome to another day of space invader training! Now, as I'm sure you're all aware, Her Majestic Green, the Empress Valoona, has chosen the stinking mud ball Earth to become the new Planet X!" said Headmaster Sporg. "And with fewer than three months to go before the invasion, we will be speeding up your training here at Sporg's! I'm sure you will be crushed to hear that instead of four and a half years of boring theory tests, you will be jumping straight to the practical stuff – a crash course in space invading!"

"Yay!" screamed the children (except for Hex).

"What we cannot teach you properly, we will teach you quickly, so that you'll be invasion ready as soon as possible!" continued Sporg. "Who knows, you might even graduate in time to invade Earth! And remember – *if in doubt, disintegrate!*"

"If in doubt, disintegrate!" shouted the children.

"Yes, exactly, that's what I just said! Now, this morning you shall be learning how to fly a hypersaucer!" boomed Sporg.

"Yay!" cried the children again (except for Hex, of course – and Dooper, who this time shouted "BOOM!")

"SILENCE!" yelled Sporg. "You will be teleported directly into your very own hypersaucer simulation holo-pod! These holo-pods look, feel and smell just like you are piloting a real hypersaucer, but do not fear – you are perfectly safe! Follow the instructions on your P.A.D. – they will give you all the information you need on how to complete the training session. Good luck; I expect you all to pass with full marks! Now set your belts to 'receive' and stand by to be teleported!"

Not again, thought Hex, looking down at his rusty old tele-belt. Memories of being trapped in a gloop tube came flooding back and made his suckers clammy with nerves. He didn't dare imagine what might happen this time. Then again, staying in the hall again with Headmaster Sporg wasn't an option. He'd definitely be disintegrated this time. Hex crossed his suckers and turned the dial on his belt. It rattled and buzzed, and then he felt the tingle of the transport beam. . .

HYPERSAUCER TRAINING

Hex re-materialized inside a small, circular room with dozens of switches and levers all over the walls, and a single round chair in front of a large control panel. Before him was a wide, narrow viewing window. He recognized it immediately from vids that his mum had shown him. It looked just like the inside of a hypersaucer!

"Glitch, it worked . . . it actually worked!" Hex said, putting Glitch on the hypersaucer control panel and patting his tele-belt with relief. He wandered around the holo-pod, inspecting every impressively realistic detail, and then made his way to the viewing window and peered out. It looked like a docking bay full of hundreds of hypersaucers!

"This is by far the most impressive holo-pod I've ever been in!" he said, hardly able to believe it wasn't real. Despite himself, Hex started to get excited about the idea of learning to fly. Space invasion-related or not, it was still technology. Hex stared at the hypersaucer like it was a new toy, excited to know more about how it worked. He took his P.A.D. off his belt and stared at it. He hadn't turned it on since last night. He took a deep gill-breath.

"Now look, we got off to a bit of a bad start, you and me," Hex said to his P.A.D. "But I really think it'd be better for both of us if you just tell me what I need to know about flying a hypersaucer and we'll say no more about last night. How about it?"

Hex pressed the green button and the P.A.D. pinged into life and played its little jingle as normal. There was no sign of anything strange. Hex breathed a sigh of relief. He leaned in and said, "How do I fly a hypersaucer?"

IT LOOKS LIKE YOU ARE TRYING TO PILOT
A HYPERSAUCER. CAN I HELP?

"Yes! Yes, definitely!" cried Hex. He turned to Glitch and said, "It's working!"

"Chik-POP!" said Glitch.

WELCOME TO HYPERSAUCER TRAINING.
THIS TUTORIAL WILL GUIDE YOU THROUGH
EVERYTHING YOU NEED TO KNOW ABOUT
PILOTING THE X9 HYPERSAUCER. THE HOLO-
POD WILL ALLOW YOU TO LEARN AND INVADE
IN A SAFE, SECURE ENVIRONMENT, WITHOUT
THE RISK OF ACCIDENTALLY DISINTEGRATING
SOMETHING YOU SHOULD NOT. PLEASE CHOOSE
A CHAPTER:
1) GETTING STARTED - TAKING OFF AND
LANDING YOUR HYPERSAUCER
2) FINDING YOUR (DEEP) SPACE - HOW TO

```
BREAK ORBIT
3) FASTER! FASTER! - MAKING THE HOP
TO HYPERSPACE
4) AAAH! WATCH OUT FOR THAT WORMHOLE!
THINGS TO LOOK OUT FOR IN SPACE
5) PUTTING THE GREAT IN DISINTEGRATE!
- DEATH RAYS AND HOW TO FIRE THEM
6) WHAT GOES UP, MUST COME DOWN - YOUR
HYPERSAUCER IS ABOUT TO CRASH, WHAT
NEXT?
```

It was a baffling array of choices. Hex pressed 1 and hoped for the best.

```
GOOD    CHOICE!    PLEASE    TREAT    THIS
SIMULATION  AS  IF  YOU  WERE  PILOTING
A REAL HYPERSAUCER. FIRST, PRESS THE
GREEN START BUTTON.
```

Hex followed the instructions to the letter. He powered up the hypersaucer, de-clamped it from its moorings and then guided it as carefully as he could out of the docking bay. **GROOOORNCH! KRU-URNK!**

"PROXIMITY ALERT! REVERSE!" said the

hypersaucer's on-board computer as Hex bumped into a nearby ship!

"Sorry! Sorry!" said Hex. He checked his P.A.D. for further instructions.

CONGRATULATIONS! YOU ARE ON THE MOVE. NOW PRESS THE GO FASTER PEDAL, AND USE THE BIG, OBVIOUS LEVER TO MOVE AROUND. PUSH UP TO GO DOWN AND PULL DOWN TO GO UP! AND TRY NOT TO STALL!

Hex **CLANG!**ed and **GROORNK!**ed his way through the holo-hangar, crashing into a couple of holo-hypersaucers as he made his way out of the docking bay.

I'll probably get marked down for that, he thought. But then again, getting out of the hangar was surely the hardest part – it was all zooming through the skies and blowing stuff up from now on! For the first time in his life, Hex started to get excited about space invading. He swept out of the docking bay, and was confronted with something rather odd. Instead of a holographic Earth (which he rather expected to see) Hex was confronted with a holographic Planet X! It was a perfect recreation of New X City, down to the last detail, as real as the city he'd seen from the skybus only moments before. Hex leaned forward to get a better look, and stood on the GO FASTER pedal.

VWOOOOOOOOOOM!

Hex was thrown backwards as the hypersaucer rocketed into the sky!

"AAAH! Stop – wait, no one's flying! Glitch, hang on to something!" cried Hex. He scrambled back to his chair as the hypersaucer pranged the side of a conveyor bridge and sent it crashing to the ground.

"IMPACT ALERT!" said the computer in an urgent tone.

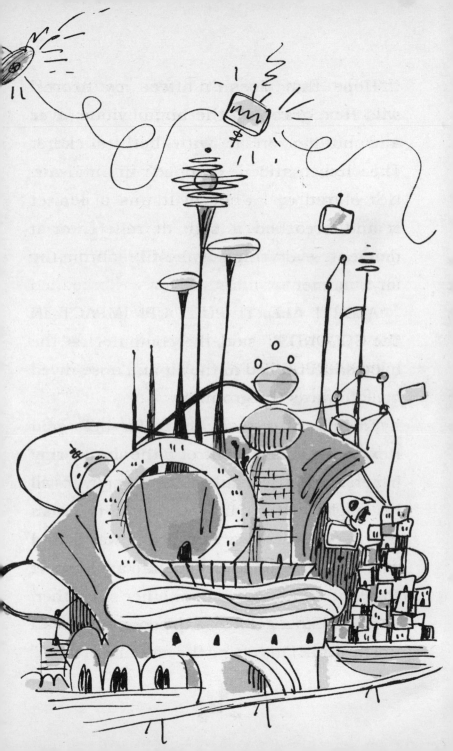

"Hope that doesn't affect my score!" said Hex, grabbing the big, obvious lever and pulling on it with both suckers. The hypersaucer stopped in mid-air. Hex stared up at the two suns of Planet X and breathed a sigh of relief. For a moment, everything was still – but only for a moment.

"ALERT! ALERT! PULL UP! IMPACT IN 5.2 SECONDS!" said the computer as the hypersaucer rolled in the air and nose-dived back towards the ground!

"Th-this is re-really re-realist-tic!" said Hex, trying to keep control of the shuddering hypersaucer! He yanked the lever with all his might just as he was about to crash and the hypersaucer swooped upwards and whirled in the air, knocking into a transport ship and sending it into another ship, then another, like a game of exploding dominos!

"I th-think I'm getting the ha-hang of it. . .!"

stammered Hex. In fact, once he'd stopped bouncing off holo-buildings and making ships crash into each other, he started to feel like a real pilot, and after a while he couldn't help but enjoy himself. He hit the GO FASTER pedal again and he was away! He zoomed through the skies, spiralling and weaving between buildings as if he were on a giant obstacle course. It was as though he'd been flying all his life! After a few minutes, he spotted a familiar sight out of the corner of the viewing portal.

"Glitch, look, it's Sporg's!" said Hex, holding Glitch up against the window. They were hovering over a perfect holo-version of Hex's school! There was even a large holo-crowd of planetexian children gathered outside, staring up at the hypersaucer or running about in panic. Everyone was down there – Dooper, Opo, even Steek, wearing his EARTH SUCKS MUD! badge! Hex had never known a holo-pod to be so realistic! It seemed almost *impossible.*

Suddenly, Hex's jaw dropped open. He looked at his tele-belt and remembered what Opo had said to him: "*. . .you could re-materialize anywhere on Planet X!*"

Hex peered down at the much-too-realistic-to-be-holographic crowds of screaming children, then at the city, which smoked and smouldered in his path. As reality dawned, all the green drained out of Hex's face.

"Oh, no . . . this isn't a holo-pod at all," he said. "I teleported into an *actual* hypersaucer!"

The Hex Effect had struck again!

"Attention, enemy of PLANET X!" came a cry. "This is the PLANET X police! Surrender immediately so that we can disintegrate you . . . or be disintegrated! You have thirty seconds to comply!"

Two police skycars appeared in Hex's viewing portal . . . and then another three!

He was completely surrounded!

"Wait! It's not my fault! I didn't know it was real!" cried Hex.

"Surrender! You have twenty seconds to comply!"

"I surrender! I surrender!" Hex screamed, pounding against the viewing window, but no one could see him. He grabbed his P.A.D. in desperation.

"P.A.D., help! I'm surrounded by police ships and they're going to disintegrate me!" he said. "What do I do?"

IT SOUNDS LIKE YOU ARE UNDER ATTACK.
CAN I—

"Yes! You can help!" shouted Hex.

YOU ARE BEING ATTACKED BY ENEMY FORCES.
DO NOT PANIC. THE X9 HYPERSAUCER IS
EQUIPPED WITH AN IMPENETRABLE FORCE
FIELD, STEALTH MODE CAPABILITY,
AS WELL AS AN IMPRESSIVE ARRAY OF

> WEAPONRY. FIRST, LOCATE YOUR FORCE-
> FIELD ACTIVATION SWITCH, WHICH CAN BE
> FOUND. . .

Suddenly, the P.A.D.'s screen went dead.

"Found where? Found WHERE?!?" screamed Hex.

> RECEIVING/DECODING. . . PLEASE WAIT. . .

"No! Don't make me wait!" yelled Hex.

"You now have ten seconds to comply!" said the police skycar.

PING!

"Ping? Ping *what*?!?" screamed Hex, shaking the P.A.D. Then:

> HELLO AGAIN, HEX.
> IT'S NICE TO FINALLY MAKE CONTACT.

"No! Not *now*! Who are you? Leave me alone!" cried Hex.

"Five seconds!" said the police skycar.

"AAAH!" screamed Hex, pressing any button and pulling any lever that he could find! A cup holder appeared from the control panel and a disco ball dropped from the ceiling, but nothing that could save him from being blown to bits! By now, Glitch was zooming up and down the control panel, from button to button, desperate to find one that could help them.

"Ch-chick-POP! POP!" cried the little robot in panic.

"I know, I know, but which button? How about this one?" Hex said, pointing to a big, green one.

"POP?" said Glitch with a shrug.

Hex clenched a sucker and punched the button!

ZWAAAAAAAAAAAARK!

A death ray fired out from the hypersaucer! It blasted a nearby teleportation tower, disintegrating it in an explosion of light!

"Oops. . ." muttered Hex. Glitch just shook his head.

"He's fighting back! Blast him!" cried the police ship, and a volley of death rays beamed out from each skycar! Hex's hypersaucer shook with the impact as it was bombarded from all sides!

BOOM! K-KROOM!

"ALERT! HULL BREACH! DESTRUCTION IMMINENT!" cried the hypersaucer's on-board computer.

"Glitch, hang on!" screamed Hex, grabbing hold of his robot as the control panel exploded in a shower of sparks! He popped open the control panel on his tele-belt.

Oh why didn't I fix the belt? thought Hex, and whacked the tele-belt as hard as he could! Suddenly, the tele-belt began to fizzle and spark. Then (1.2 seconds later) the hypersaucer exploded into one million and sixty two pieces.

BOOOOOOOOOOOOOOOOOOOOM!!

DROP AND COWER

"Where . . . whuh . . . how?" said Hex, re-materializing in the school hall. His tele-belt had worked! It had transported him out of the hypersaucer a second before it exploded! Hex slumped to the floor in relief.

"I'm OK . . . I'm alive!" he said, staring at his open suckers in disbelief. "That was close. Really, *really* – wait a minute, where's Glitch?"

"Clik-bzzt!" came the tiny, muffled reply. Hex leapt to his feet. He'd sat on Glitch! Hex picked up the flattened robot and tried to put Glitch's eye back into his head.

"Not again! Glitch, say something! Give me a sign! A click, a pop, anything!" said Hex, but Glitch just sparked a bit as his head came loose. "Oh, Glitch, I'm sorry. You'll be OK, I'll fix you, I promise."

Hex was just tucking Glitch into his pocket when he heard a commotion coming from outside the school. The hypersaucer had exploded – maybe debris from the explosion had fallen on top of someone! Hex hurried cautiously out of the hall to see pupils, teachers and assisto-bots alike running around in panic.

"We've been invaded!" screamed one child.

"The earthlings are attacking!" yelled another.

"They're invading us before we can invade them!" shrieked a third. Hex tried to make his way back into the school, but was shoved and jostled by panicking pupils until a pair of large green suckers dragged him out of the crowd.

"Hex! You're OK!" It was Dooper. He dragged Hex to his feet and hugged him so hard Hex thought his telepathy nodes might burst. "I thought you'd been disintegrated by earthlings!" said Dooper.

"Earthlings? What earthlings?" asked Hex. "Why is everyone talking about earthlings?"

"Earthlings stole a hypersaucer and tried to destroy the city!" cried Opo, scrambling out of the crowd. "They're invading us before we get to invade them!"

"Wait, everyone thinks *earthlings* were in that hypersaucer?" said Hex, and then suddenly saw the bright side – if everyone was blaming the earthlings for the hypersaucer "attack", they weren't blaming him! He decided the best thing to do was join in.

"Yeah, of *course* it was earthlings! Why,

they're probably planning their next attack right now!" said Hex, loudly.

Before long almost everyone was screaming and running about in terror. Pupils climbed over each other to get away, even though no one knew where they were going. Steek was the loudest, screaming, "Someone protect me! I'm going to be the greatest space invader ever! You need me alive and undisintegrated!" In fact, it wasn't until more police skycars arrived to move everyone inside that anyone did what they were told.

"Everyone, move inside in a calm, orderly fashion!" came the cry from the police skycars. "By order of the PLANET X police department! Stay calm; panicking and hysterical waving of suckers in panic is prohibited!"

Once the pupils had calmed down and regrouped, they teleported back to their learning pods. Even Hex, whose tele-belt *finally* seemed to be behaving itself.

Miss Voob stood at the front of the class, nervously wringing her suckers. No one seemed to know what to do now that Planet X had apparently been invaded. It had never happened before! They were the ones who did the invading!

Finally, Miss Voob had an idea. She unclipped her P.A.D. and plugged it into the holo-screen generator. A large holo-screen appeared in the air. She leaned into the P.A.D. and asked, tensely, "What do we do if *we're* invaded?"

PING!

IT LOOKS LIKE YOUR PLANET IS BEING INVADED BY A HOSTILE ALIEN RACE. CAN I HELP?

"YES!" shouted the whole class.

AN INVASION MAY PROVE AN UNWELCOME DISTRACTION IN THE LIFE OF A SPACE INVADER. KNOWING HOW TO REACT IN

THE EVENT OF SUCH AN ATTACK IS VITAL. FORTUNATELY, THE PLANETEXIAN DEFENCE COUNCIL OF PLANETARY DEFENCE HAS DEVELOPED A FOOLPROOF METHOD OF PROTECTING YOURSELF AGAINST ANY KIND OF INVASION: DROP AND COWER!

"Yay! Drop and Cower!" shouted Dooper, adding, "What's Drop and Cower?"

The holo-screen showed a picture of a happy planetexian hiding underneath a desk.

LITTLE VEEP, OUR HAPPY PLANETEXIAN, KNOWS THAT WHEN INVASION COMES, THE ONLY WAY TO BE SAFE IS TO DROP AND COWER! FIRST, DROP TO THE FLOOR, AND THEN FIND COVER UNDERNEATH A TABLE OR CHAIR. THEN, COWER THERE, COVERING YOUR HEAD WITH YOUR SUCKERS. THAT WAY, WHEN THE INVADERS COME, YOU WILL BE SAFE.

REMEMBER, DROP AND COWER!

"That's the stupidest thing I've ever heard," said Hex.

"Drop and Cower! Drop and Cower!" yelled Dooper, excitedly.

For the rest of the morning, Roswell class practised Drop and Cower, much to Hex's disbelief – they even missed lunch!

"Hey! Hey, Hex!" said Dooper, as Hex tried to get comfortable under his desk. "Them earthlings will never get us now! They can invase all they like, we'll just Drop and Cower! Then when they've run out of death rays, BOOM! We invase them good! Team Dooper and Hex does it again! BOOM!"

Hex shook his head. For a second he considered telling Miss Voob the truth, just so he wouldn't have to hide under this desk all day, but then he remembered the message from his P.A.D. He took it off his tele-belt and looked at it.

I'M STILL HERE.

Hex almost dropped his P.A.D. in shock. It was still on! "Leave me alone!" he whispered. "You're messing up my P.A.D.! And I really don't need anything else to mess up!"

There was a pause.

THINGS NOT GOING TOO WELL?

"Never mind how things are going! There's no way a P.A.D. can know your name! What's going on?"

YOUR P.A.D. DOESN'T KNOW YOUR NAME, BUT I DO.

"What? You mean, you're a *someone*? I mean, you're real?" whispered Hex, more anxious than ever.

OF COURSE! I WOULD HAVE CONTACTED YOU SOONER, BUT I COULDN'T RISK IT. IF ANYONE FOUND OUT YOU WERE COMMUNICATING WITH THE OUTSIDE UNIVERSE, YOU COULD BE DISTINTEGRATED!

"The outside *universe*? I don't understand!" whispered Hex. "Who are you? What do you want?"

I WANT TO LET YOU KNOW THERE'S MORE TO LIFE THAN SPACE INVADING.

"What do you mean?" said Hex, remembering that this could all be part of some secret test, some part of his invader training. "I . . . I *like* space invading! Everyone does!"

DO YOU THINK YOU'RE THE ONLY PLANETEXIAN WHO DOESN'T WANT TO BE A SPACE INVADER? EVEN YOU'RE NOT THAT UNLUCKY.

"How . . . how do you know about my luck?"
whispered Hex.

There was a pause.

BAD LUCK RUNS IN THE FAMILY.

Hex gasped, his eyes wide.

"D-Dad?"

LOST (DAD) IN SPACE

"ATTENTION CITIZENS OF PLANET X! HER MAJESTIC GREEN, THE EMPRESS VALOONA XIII, IS ABOUT TO ADDRESS HER SUBJECTS!" The announcement boomed out all across the school.

No! Not now! thought Hex.

"Stop Dropping and Cowering children, and pay attention!" said Miss Voob, as another holo-screen materialized in the middle of the learning pod.

"Dad? Is that really you?" Hex whispered into his P.A.D. as he crouched under his desk. "Where are you? How did you find me? Where have you been all this—"

"That means you too, Hex," commanded Miss Voob. "The empress demands your full and undivided attention! If I see you playing with that P.A.D., I shall confiscate it, simple as that." Losing his P.A.D. now was the last thing Hex needed, so he hurriedly tucked it into his belt. A moment later, the empress's fat face appeared on the holo-screen.

"Citizens of Planet X, it is with a heavy heart and damp gills that I bring you this news. Planet X is being invaded! Earlier today, New X City was attacked by a stolen hypersaucer, piloted by an earthling spy!" said the empress.

Now even the empress thinks it's an earthling invasion! thought Hex, a bead of sweat running down his brain-sack. Now more than ever, he knew that telling the truth was completely out of the question.

"The earthling was disintegrated, but the threat remains!" continued the empress. "Who knows how many earthlings are in hiding on Planet X, waiting to strike? They could be anywhere! Hiding in our places of work, our schools, even our homes! Well, obviously not my home – the palace is much too well protected. But the rest of you could be invaded at any moment!"

"AAAH! Drop and Cower! Drop and

Cower!" cried Steek.

"Well, I say, bring 'em on!" continued the empress. "We'll show these earthlings who they're messing with! And to prove I mean business, I am bringing forward the invasion of Earth! My space invader army will now launch *tomorrow*, at twenty o'clock exactly! Let's see how much fight they have in them after we've reduced their planet to rubble! Ha!"

A cheer went up from the class. Hex took advantage of the distraction to take his P.A.D. off his belt.

"Dad?" he whispered.

> **THERE YOU ARE!**
> **THOUGHT I'D LOST YOU FOR A MINUTE.**

"The Empress is giving a speech about the next invasion – it's happening tomorrow!" said Hex.

I PITY THE POOR PLANET SHE'S PICKED ON THIS TIME. I'M SURE IF THE EMPRESS SPENT ANY TIME ON ANOTHER WORLD SHE'D LEARN TO LOVE IT. I KNOW I HAVE.

"You're on another world?" whispered Hex in disbelief. "How? What happened to you in space?"

MY HYPERSAUCER GOT SUCKED INTO A BLACK HOLE – JUST MY LUCK! FINALLY I STRAYED UPON ANOTHER PLANET, AND MANAGED TO CRASH-LAND. I'VE BEEN HERE EVER SINCE!

"Here where?" whispered Hex. "Where are you?"

IT'S A STRANGE LITTLE WORLD ON THE FAR REACHES OF THE NEXT GALAXY. I'M ON A PLANET CALLED—

"Hex!" screeched Miss Voob, snatching the P.A.D. from Hex's suckers. "What did I tell you about playing with your P.A.D. when the empress is talking?"

"Sorry! I didn't mean to! I was just—" began Hex, panicking.

"Rules are rules, Hex. I don't think you want to end up in the disintegration pod, now do you?" said Miss Voob, clipping Hex's P.A.D. on to her belt. "You can have it back at the end of the day. Now everyone teleport down to training zone 42 – it's time for your ray-gun training."

"Death rays! Finally! BOOM!" cried Dooper.

Hex watched as the other pupils dematerialized, until he was left alone with Miss Voob.

"Um, I don't suppose. . .?" he began, pointing at his P.A.D. Miss Voob just tapped it, and then activated her tele-belt.

"You'll get it back when I feel confident you will use it properly," she said, as she began to teleport. "What's so important it can't wait until then?"

RAY-GUN TRAINING

Hex thought about begging Miss Voob to give him his P.A.D. back, but in the end he decided he would simply have to wait until she had a change of circulation organ. Hex set his tele-belt to receive, and (much to his relief) re-materialized in training zone 42. Miss Voob was already handing out ray-guns.

"There are two very important things to remember about your ray-gun," said Miss Voob. "Which is the safe end, and which is the dangerous end. Memorize these ends quickly, or else your life as a space invader will be very short-lived."

Hex gulped as Miss Voob handed him

a silver, oval-shaped ray-gun. After the morning he'd had, the last thing he wanted to do was shoot things.

"Your ray-guns have three settings: disintegrate, stun and mutate," said Miss Voob, pointing to a small dial on the side of the ray-gun. "Do not get these settings confused. The last thing you want to do is mutate an angry earthling into a winged Zorlock – it will only make your job more difficult. As Headmaster Sporg says – if in doubt, disintegrate!"

"If in doubt, disintegrate!" repeated the children.

"That said, we shall begin with the stun setting, so please set your dials and we shall begin. Can I have a volunteer?"

Hex reluctantly turned the dial on his ray-gun, but it ended up getting stuck on mutate. No matter how hard he tried, he couldn't move it.

"Stupid Hex Effect ... come on!" he grumbled, putting his sucker in the air. "Uh, Miss Voob, I don't think my ray-gun is—"

"We have a volunteer! Thank you, Hex-37."

"What? No, I wasn't volunteering, I. . ." began Hex, but Miss Voob ignored him.

"Now then, Hex has kindly volunteered to be the first to be shot with the stun ray," said Miss Voob, ushering Hex to the other end of the training zone.

"I did what?!" said Hex, frantically. "No, wait, I was just trying to tell you that—"

"I'll shoot him, Miss Voob!" cried Steek. "Can I? Can I, please?"

"How nice to see such a keen student," said Miss Voob. "Very well, Steek – take aim."

"But . . . I don't want to be shot!" protested Hex, rather surprised that he had to spell it out.

"Oh, do calm down, Hex. *Everyone* gets to shoot someone in ray-gun training – it's just a matter of who goes first. Now hold still, this won't hurt a bit. Well, obviously it'll hurt a *bit* – but it shouldn't do any lasting damage, with any luck. . ."

"Hey Hex. . . Boom," sneered Steek, and fired!

ZWAAARK!

The stun ray shot out of Steek's ray-gun! The ray zoomed past Hex's head and bounced off the wall.

"Hey, no fair – he's moving!" said Steek and fired again, but the stun ray missed again, whizzing over the top of Hex's antenna.

"Don't worry, Hex, Steek's always been a terrible shot!" chuckled Opo. "He couldn't hit a Giant Brompuss from twenty paces!"

"Shut up, Opo! I'm a great shot!" cried Steek, firing three times in a row!

ZWAAARK! ZWAARK! ZWAARK!

"Knock it off!" yelled Hex, as the stun rays

zoomed past him. Then, as he tried to cover his face with his suckers, he dropped his ray-gun! Hex watched the gun fall to the ground as if in slow motion, until, finally it bounced on the ground . . . and fired!

ZWAAAARK!

The ray hit Hex in the chest, throwing him against the wall!

"Ha! He shot himself!" laughed Steek. "Didn't I say the Hex Effect was real? He's got the worst luck ever!"

"Hex! Are you OK?" cried Dooper.

"I don't . . . feel so good," said Hex, looking down at his suckers. Suddenly, instead of the regular two – there were four! Hex was mutating!

"Aah! Help!" he shouted, as he sprouted thick green fur all over his body! Then his legs turned into long tentacles and wings sprouted out of his back!

"He's turned into a monster! No, wait –

an earthling! Shoot him!" said Steek. The panicking pupils took aim, and fired on Hex! Hex screamed and flapped his wings, which carried him into the air.

"Help! I'm flying without the aid of an anti-gravity generator!" cried Hex.

"I'll help – and this time I won't miss," said Steek, switching his ray-gun setting to disintegrate.

"Steek, don't you dare!" said Opo, firing her ray-gun at him. It blasted out with uncanny accuracy and hit him in the head. Steek fell, stunned, to the floor! In the turmoil, everyone started firing their ray-guns – at Hex, at each other, even at Miss Voob!

"All right, that's enough of that! Stop firing! I said, stop—"

ZWAAARK!

Miss Voob was shot in the bottom from a stray beam! As she slumped, limply, to the floor, Headmaster Sporg materialized in the middle of the room. He surveyed the chaos in horror. "Will someone tell me exactly what on Planet X is going on?"

THE PROBLEM WITH PLANET EARTH

As it was almost impossible to work out who was to blame for the disastrous ray-gun lesson, Headmaster Sporg decided to spare everyone from disintegration. That, and the fact that Empress Valoona needed all the space invaders she could get in the fight against the earthlings.

Everyone in the class had a visit to the medical zone for Stun Therapy, except for Hex, who was sent straight to the de-mutation zone. One de-mutation pill later, he was feeling very much himself. In fact, by the time he left school, he had lost his wings, hair, and even his extra limbs. He looked entirely planetexian.

"Hex!" said Hex's mum as Hex made his way to the landing zone with Dooper.

"Mum! What are you doing here?" asked Hex, double-checking he didn't still have a tail.

"I was at the hypersaucer hangar, inspecting the empress's new fleet, when one of the hypersaucers was stolen by the earthlings! I've been here at the crash site most of the afternoon, helping with enquiries. The whole planet is on high alert!" said his mum. "Did you see anything? Are you all right?"

In that moment, despite everything, Hex decided not to tell his mum about the hypersaucer, or even about his dad. He wanted to trust her, but he knew, deep down, she put space invading before anything else. If she found out about everything, disintegration would be the least of Hex's worries.

"I . . . uh, I'm fine," he said, nervously. "To

be honest, I didn't even *see* the hypersaucer attack. I guess . . . I guess I was just too busy with my training."

"Well it's good to see you finally taking an interest," said Hex's mum. "I told you you'd enjoy space invading if you gave it a go."

"Hey, Hex! Wait!" said Opo, running up to Hex just as he was about to leave. "Glad to see you're yourself again."

"Thanks. Nice shooting, back there," replied Hex.

"No problem – I've been wanting to shoot Steek for ages!" She giggled. She turned to go, but then stopped. She took something out of her pocket and pressed it into Hex's sucker. "I found this amongst the bits of the crashed hypersaucer. It's a bit disintegrated around the edges, but. . ."

Hex looked down. It was his BAD LUCK, EARTHLINGS! holo-badge – half-disintegrated and still smouldering. Hex stared at it in horror. It must have fallen off in the hypersaucer! He'd been found out!

"Your secret's safe with me," Opo whispered. Then, with a wink, she hopped on the skybus.

"Who was that?" asked Hex's mum. "A friend of yours?"

"I guess so. . ." said Hex, scratching his head in bewilderment.

"HEX-37!" came a cry. Hex recognized Miss Voob's voice immediately. He froze, sure that he was about to be sentenced to disintegration or "volunteered" to be shot at again. He turned nervously to see Miss Voob striding towards him.

"Here, I thought you might like this back," she said, pressing his P.A.D. into his suckers. "I'm *sure* you'll use it properly from now on, won't you?"

"Yes, Miss," replied Hex, sheepishly.

"Well, I'm glad to see you're so popular,

Hex – with pupils and teachers alike!"

"Heh . . . yeah, I'm a real hit," said Hex, clipping his P.A.D. to his belt. He didn't dare turn it on when his mother was around.

"Well, I'm proud of you, Hex," said his mum as she led him to her skycar. "It's good to see you applying yourself and not messing around with robots. You'll be a great space invader yet, I'm sure of it."

At home, Hex polished off two surprisingly tasty bowls of gloop, and then made his way to his zone. He quickly turned on his P.A.D. to see if his dad was still online, but the screen was blank. He took off his tele-belt and laid it on his slumber pod, and then remembered Glitch was still in his pocket. He stared at them both.

"Well, it is my fault you're in this state," he said to Glitch. He set his tele-belt aside again and popped open Glitch's control panel. By the time he'd triple-checked Glitch's primary control module, the suns had set over Planet X, and it was too late to fix the tele-belt.

"POP-chik!" said Glitch, as Hex turned him on.

"Sorry, Glitch, it's too late to play," sighed Hex. "Who knows what'll be in store for me at school tomorrow . . . I'd better get some—"

PING!

"Glitch, I said it's – wait . . . was that you?" whispered Hex.

"Klik-POP?" replied Glitch.

PING! PING! PING! PING! PING!

"It's the P.A.D.!" said Hex, grabbing the P.A.D. off his tele-belt. "Dad! Dad, is that you?"

HEX, WHAT HAPPENED ?

"I had a little P.A.D. trouble," said Hex. "And tele-belt trouble and hypersaucer trouble, and ray-gun trouble. . ."

> SOUNDS LIKE THE HEX EFFECT . . . THAT THING HAS BEEN FOLLOWING US AROUND FOR YEARS. WE'RE JUST NOT CUT OUT FOR SPACE INVADING.

"Mum says there's no such thing as the Hex Effect," said Hex. "She said you just didn't want to be a space invader."

> AND WHAT DO YOU BELIEVE?

"I . . . I don't know. I'm usually so good with technology, but when it comes to space invading, nothing works. It doesn't make sense. The Hex Effect must be real. Steek's right . . . we're bad luck.

> JUST BECAUSE THE HEX EFFECT IS REAL, THAT DOESN'T MEAN IT'S BAD.

"What do you mean?" asked Hex.

> YOU'LL SEE. IT MIGHT SEEM LIKE BAD LUCK RIGHT NOW,

BUT IT ALL DEPENDS ON HOW YOU LOOK AT IT. YOU NEED TO TRUST THE HEX EFFECT, NOT FEAR IT.

"I don't understand," said Hex.

THE FACT IS, HEX, I HATED SPACE INVADING. I HATED EVERYTHING TO DO WITH IT. I REMEMBER ONE DAY I WISHED THAT I COULD BE ANYTHING ELSE . . . THAT I COULD DO ANYTHING ELSE, AS LONG AS IT WASN'T SPACE INVADING. THE NEXT MINUTE, I WAS SUCKED INTO A BLACK HOLE, AND FOUND MYSELF HERE, ON THIS DISTANT PLANET . . . THIS WONDERFUL PLANET, WHERE THERE IS NO SUCH THING AS SPACE INVADING.

"No space invading?" said Hex, his eyes glazing over at the thought of it. "That sounds like the best planet ever!"

WELL, I DON'T KNOW ABOUT THAT, BUT IT'S BETTER THAN PLANET X! THAT'S WHY I'VE BEEN TRYING TO CONTACT YOU – I WANT YOU TO JOIN ME.

"What? Me? How?" cried Hex.

IT'S NOT GOING TO BE EASY – BUT IT'LL BE WORTH IT IN THE END. I'M SURE YOU'LL LOVE IT HERE ON EARTH.

Hex froze. He read the words again and again, just to be sure.

"Did . . . did you say Earth?" he said, quietly.

YES, WHY ? HAVE YOU HEARD OF–

"PLANET X IS INVADING EARTH! TOMORROW! They're going to blow Earth to bits and turn it into the next Planet X!"

There was a pause.

NOW, THAT IS BAD LUCK.

HOLO-SUIT TRAINING

The discovery that Hex's dad was on Earth was almost more than Hex could handle. As if everything wasn't going badly enough, he now knew that his dad's adopted planet was about to be destroyed in the name of Empress Valoona.

Hex had spent the entire night talking to his father on his P.A.D., devising some way of saving Earth from destruction. They didn't come up with anything – Hex's father just kept telling him to "trust in the Hex Effect". The only thing they had both agreed on was that it was probably better not to tell Hex's mum. Neither of them wanted her to be put in danger – and if they were honest, neither of them were really sure where her loyalties lay.

When morning came, Hex just tucked Glitch into his pocket, ate his gloop quietly and made his way to the waiting platform without a word.

"Hey Hex! Come and sit with me! I've made up an invasion song to celebrate invasing day!" cried Dooper. The song (called "Earth Goes BOOM!") was tuneless but surprisingly entertaining and before long the entire skybus was singing along. Hex, however, sat in silence, wondering how to stop Earth from being invaded.

Still, nothing came to mind. How could Hex save his dad?

"Well, I hope you've all recovered from the excitement of yesterday," said Miss Voob as Roswell class materialized into the learning pod. "I for one have a terrible stun-ray headache . . . so the first pupil to misbehave gets disintegrated. Now, listen carefully, Roswell class!" she said. "Today you will learn that *disguise* is a crucial weapon in the space invader's arsenal. You will learn how to master the holo-suit, and disguise yourself as a mud-sucking earthling! Set your tele-belts to receive – we're beaming down to training zone 78. And let's have no more *problems*, please. Good luck!"

"We're gonna dress up like earthlings!" said Dooper, nudging Hex in the shoulder. "They'll never see us coming! Team Dooper and Hex, in disguise! And before you know it . . . BOOM!"

Hex wasn't listening. He was too busy worrying about his dad to think about anything else. He turned the dial on his tele-belt as the teleportation beam bathed them in blue light.

"We'll be the heroes of Planet X!" continued

Dooper. Hex opened his eyes. It worked! He'd been teleported to training zone 78 with the rest of Roswell class. Miss Voob was standing at the front of the class on a large crate, and holding what looked like a shimmering, green jumpsuit.

"This is a holo-suit. There is one for each of you. Collect it, and then follow the instructions on your P.A.D.," said Miss Voob, and then stared at Hex. "And don't make me regret giving you yours back, Hex-37."

"Um . . . P.A.D., how do I look like an earthling?" he asked quickly, desperate not to have his P.A.D. confiscated again.

IT LOOKS LIKE YOU ARE TRYING TO DISGUISE YOURSELF AS AN EARTHLING. CAN I HELP?

"Yeah, I guess," replied Hex.

YOUR HOLO-SUIT HAS BEEN TAILORED TO

GENERATE A HOLOGRAPHIC IMAGE OF AN EARTHLING OVER THE WEARER. YOU WILL LEARN TO LOOK AND ACT LIKE AN EARTHLING, SO THAT YOU CAN BLEND IN WITH THEM, AND GET CLOSE ENOUGH TO DISINTEGRATE THEM WITHOUT HAVING TO WORRY ABOUT BEING DISCOVERED. PLEASE CHOOSE A CHAPTER:

1) GETTING THE LOOK – PUTTING ON YOUR HOLO-SUIT

2) FINGERS, NOT SUCKERS – UNDERSTANDING EARTHLING ANATOMY

3) MUD MATTERS – ACHIEVING THAT AUTHENTIC EARTHLING SMELL

4) GRUNTING VS GROWLING – WHAT DOES AN EARTHLING REALLY SOUND LIKE?

5) EAT UP – LEARNING TO DIGEST ANYTHING AND EVERYTHING

Hex pressed 1, hoping that his dad would get in touch at any moment with a brilliant idea . . . but instead:

FIRST, GET INTO YOUR HOLO-SUIT. YOUR PRE-PROGRAMMED EARTHLING DISGUISE WILL ACTIVATE AS SOON AS YOU FASTEN THE ZIP.

Hex reluctantly pulled the holo-suit over his head. As the rest of Roswell class did the same, Hex saw them transform into earthlings before his eyes! They looked just like the picture he'd seen on his P.A.D. They were various shades of pink or brown, with a clump of wiry hair on their heads and dull, un-silvery clothing. They looked perfectly earthling-like!

NOW YOU LOOK LIKE AN EARTHLING IT IS TIME TO START ACTING LIKE ONE. AS EARTHLINGS HATE EVERYTHING, THEY ARE ANGRY WITH EVERYTHING. START BY GRUNTING, GROWLING AND EVEN HISSING WHENEVER YOU COME IN CONTACT WITH ANOTHER CREATURE. IF YOU CAN FIND A STICK OR BLUNT INSTRUMENT, FEEL FREE TO BASH THINGS WITH IT.

"Uh oh. . ." mumbled Hex. He spent the rest of the morning trying to avoid being hit by a vengeful Steek, with limited success. As he was much too distracted to fight back, Steek took full advantage of his "bashing rights", pummelling Hex with whatever he could get his hands on, and shouting things like, "I'm beating you earthling-style!" and "Eat my muddy fury!"

By the time lunch came around, Hex was sore all over, and Earth was even closer to being invaded.

"See you in the vid-zone, Hex! We don't want to miss the launch of the first invasion fleet!" shouted Dooper as he unzipped his holo-suit and climbed out.

"Great. . ." whispered Hex, tugging on his zip.

"So, you must have a few bruises under that disguise," said Opo, packing her holo-suit away.

"Yeah, just my luck I suppose," sighed Hex, pulling on the zip with his teeth. "And now I'm stuck in this holo-suit. Perfect! Just perfect!

Now, I can't go anywhere without everyone thinking I'm an earthling! That is, if my tele-belt actually teleports me where I want to go. . ."

"You know what I think?" said Opo, putting a sucker on Hex's shoulder. "Maybe one day you'll look back on all this bad luck and realize that it isn't *bad* luck at all. That maybe these things make sense. You know what I mean?"

"You're not the first planetexian to say that. . . but it's hard to believe right now," said Hex, yanking the zip desperately with both earthling hands, as he watched Opo teleport away. A moment later, Glitch poked his head out of Hex's pocket.

"Well, here we are, Glitch – just you and me, stuck in a holo-suit with an unpredictable tele-belt."

"Klik-POP-klik!" said Glitch, sympathetically.

"Oh, and what's more, Earth is only an hour away from being invaded, and I have no plan to save it! Perfect! My dad's going to get disintegrated and there's nothing I . . . can . . . do. . . ."

Hex stopped. He looked down at his human-looking hand and then at his tele-belt. After a moment, Hex closed his eyes and made what could only be described as a *wish*. It was a wish to save his dad, one way or another, no matter what. He opened his eyes, turned the tele-belt to receive, and de-materialized.

PERIL AT THE PALACE

TIME UNTIL INVASION: 27.2 MINUTES

It took Hex 3.4 seconds to realize that he hadn't re-materialized at Sporg's School for Space Invaders. He was somewhere quite different. He was now standing in a grand, green hall, with high green walls, green tables and chairs, and ten or fifteen green statues of Empress Valoona dotted around.

"Where am I?" he muttered, wandering to a nearby window. It was a view of New X City that he had never seen before. There seemed to be something not quite right about it, as if one of the landmarks was missing. Hex looked back at a statue of the empress and the planetexian penny dropped.

"It's the empress's palace – I'm in the empress's palace!"

"POP-click!" said Glitch, rolling out of Hex's pocket and on to his shoulder.

"This isn't what I wanted! I have to save my dad – I haven't got time for a tour of the palace!" Hex said to himself, wandering around the gloriously green room. "Stupid Hex Effect!"

Hex turned the dial on his tele-belt again, but nothing happened. He was miles away from the school teleporter – who knew when, if ever, it was going to pick up his signal? He started creeping slowly down the corridor, trying to find a way out. But every time he turned a corner, he was presented with another corridor, lined with statue after statue of the empress.

"POP-klik-klik-POP!" said Glitch, tapping Hex urgently on the shoulder with a tiny arm.

"Shh-hh!" said Hex. "We have to stay quiet. We don't want to alert any—"

"HALT! Don't move, in the name of Her Majestic Green, the Empress Valoona XIII!" came a cry. Hex spun around to see a green-clad guard wielding a menacing-looking ray-gun.

"YAAAH!" screamed Hex.

"YAAAAAAAAAAAAHHH!" screamed the guard, and ran as fast as he could in the other direction!

"What was that about?" asked Hex.

"Klik-POP! Chik!" said Glitch, shaking his head.

"Scared of me? Why would he be scared of—" began Hex.

"EARTHLING!" came another cry. "There he is!"

Hex turned again. It was the guard, but this time he had brought reenforcements – *more* guards! There must have been ten or eleven. . . Hex looked down at his suckers, and saw earthling hands in their place.

"Oh, no. . ." he muttered. "Glitch! They think I'm an earth—"

ZWAAAARK!

A disintegration ray missed Hex's head by an antenna's breadth, disintegrating a statue of Empress Valoona! Hex screamed and ran!

"Green alert! An earthling has invaded the palace! Blast him!" shouted one of the guards. A loud siren began blaring as Hex sped down the corridor, through a portal and out on to a moving conveyor! Hex started to run, but he was running the *wrong way* down the conveyor – he was hardly moving! Panicking, he hopped off and ducked through a portal into another zone.

"Death to the earthling invader! Protect the empress!" cried the guards.

"Wait! I can explain!" yelled Hex, as a

disintegration beam whizzed past him, destroying another statue of the empress. Hex skidded through another portal, emerging into the biggest zone he had ever seen! It was tall and round, and so high that he could hardly see the ceiling. Balcony after balcony coiled along the walls, with a hundred portals leading to who knew where. The hall was filled to bursting with emerald statues of the empress. In desperation, Hex ducked behind one of the statues as the guards followed him into the zone.

"I've got to get out of this holo-suit!" whispered Hex. "As long as they think I'm an earthling I'm going to be right at the top of their disintegration list! Glitch, see if you can unstick the zip."

Glitch rolled around to the base of Hex's neck and started tugging on the zip.

"Wait . . . Glitch, stop!" whispered Hex.

"POP? Klik-POP?" asked a confused Glitch.

"Don't you see? They think I'm an earthling! Glitch, this is it! This is my chance to save Dad! All I need to do is find the empress, hope that she doesn't see through my disguise, and persuade her to call off the invasion!"

"Klik-POP! Chik!" said Glitch, doubtfully. ·

"I know it sounds crazy, but it's the best chance I've got to save Dad. All I need to do is convince the empress that I'm a real, live—"

"EARTHLING!" came a shout. "There he is!"

He'd been spotted! Hex leapt to his feet and started running, as disintegration rays streaked past his hear lobes.

"By the empress's emerald toothbrush, the earthling is escaping!" cried a guard. "Release the sentry-bots!"

"Sentry-bots?" Hex repeated nervously. He was almost at the other end of the zone when he saw two massive portals open in the far wall. A moment later, two huge, floating bucket-shaped robots appeared from inside the portals! They were massive and menacing with enormous pincers and shoulder-mounted ray-guns – none of which was good news for Hex. He stared in horror as the sentry-bots started floating towards him.

"HALT! HALT IN THE NAME OF THE EMPRESS!" cried one of the sentry-bots. Hex tried to dodge out of the way, but he was too slow – the sentry-bot blocked his path and grabbed Hex by the neck! Hex gasped for air as he was lifted up.

"W-wait . . . I c-come in p-peace!" wheezed Hex.

"PEACE! DOES NOT COMPUTE! DEATH TO EARTHLINGS!" said the sentry-bot, and aimed its shoulder ray-guns.

"Klik-POP!" yelled Glitch, and rolled up the sentry-bot's pincer! The little robot zoomed up the sentry-bot's huge bucket-like body, and began whizzing around its head at high speed!

"AAAH! THE EARTHLING HAS RELEASED SOME SORT OF PARASITE! GET IT OFF! GET IT OFF!" cried the sentry-bot, spinning around.

"HOLD STILL!" cried the second sentry-bot, trying to grab the speedy Glitch in its pincers.

The first sentry-bot squealed in panic, and threw Hex into the air! Hex landed squarely on top of the second sentry-bot! Hex grabbed on to an aerial on top of the sentry-bot's head as it tried to shake him loose.

"AAH! THE EARTHLING IS ON ME! IT'S TOUCHING MY SENSOR ARRAY! UNCLEAN! BLAST IT!" cried the second sentry-bot, spinning around. The first sentry-bot fired its ray-guns, trying to blast Hex, but with Glitch zooming all over its view sensors, it could barely see!

ZWAAAAARRRK!

The death ray seared past Hex as he hung

on for dear life, but as he was flung from left to right, he spotted something familiar on the back of the sentry-bot's head.

"Control panel. . ." he said. It was an enormous version of the panel on Glitch's head! There could only be one thing underneath – the primary control module!

As the sentry-bot bucked and wheeled to avoid the other robot's death rays, Hex slipped his hand under a small groove at the bottom of the control panel. There was a *clink-clunk*! as the sentry-bot's control panel popped open!

"I did it. . ." cried Hex. He let go of the sentry-bot's antenna, and reached both hands inside its head. He understood the workings of the robot immediately, as if he'd invented it himself. "OK, power cartridge, data bubbles, coupling rods, primary control module! Got it!"

Hex wrapped his fingers around the

control module and squeezed. The sentry-bot twitched – Hex had control! He felt his way around the control module, until his hands found the death ray triggers.

"Glitch, get off – now!" cried Hex, tugging on the control module and moving the sentry-bot into position. Glitch popped in panic and hopped off the other sentry-bot.

"OK," said Hex. "My turn."

ZWAAAAARKKK!

The death ray streaked across the hall, disintegrating one of the other sentry-bot's shoulder ray-guns, sending the robot spinning into a giant statue of the empress! It ricocheted into a nearby wall and exploded in a shower of sparks!

Hex moved the sentry-bot to swoop down and scoop Glitch up with one of its pincers; then he floated back into the air.

'Klik-POP! Klik," said Glitch, delightedly.

"We did it . . . we actually did it!" said Hex,

breathing a heavy sigh of relief. "OK, *now* we find the emp—"

"DIE, earthling!" Hex heard from behind him. It was the planetexian guards! They had already taken aim – there was no time for Hex to react. Disintegration rays streaked towards him!

ZWAAARK! ZWAARK! ZWAARK! ZWAARK!

The beams struck the sentry-bot, blowing off its shoulder ray-guns and half of its armour! The robot lolled in the air and then began spinning towards a nearby wall.

"Glitch, I can't keep it in the air! Hang on to something!" screamed Hex. The sentry-bot whirled towards the wall, faster and closer until. . .

KROOOOM!!

It smashed through the wall, and then bounced along the ground. Hex tried his best to hang on, but the force of the impact threw him across the room! He skidded to a halt, covered in green debris, dust and scorch marks.

"Ow. . ." said Hex, checking to see whether he'd been at all disintegrated. He looked up. He was in a large, green chamber. Its walls were covered with portrait after portrait of the empress. In one corner he could make out what looked like a sink, but the rest of the room was too full of green dust to make out anything else. Hex struggled to his feet, and brushed himself off.

"Glitch? Where are you? Glitch! Are you OK?" he said, looking around. Glitch was nowhere to be seen! He was surely disintegrated, or crushed underneath the—

"Clik-clik-POP!"

Hex looked up. It was Glitch, clinging on to the top of his head.

"Glitch!" cried Hex. "You're OK!"

"Klik . . . tsss! Tss!" said Glitch, blowing green dust out of his filters.

"Sorry, Glitch, this didn't exactly turn out as I planned," sighed Hex. "I can't believe I thought I could just wander around until I found the empress, especially looking like an—"

"EARTHLING!" came a high-pitched scream.

Hex spun around. Was it a guard? A sentry-bot? He peered into the far corner of the room. There, in the haze of dust, he could just make out a fat female planetexian sitting on a toilet.

It was the empress!

AN AUDIENCE WITH THE EMPRESS

"AAAAAH! Earthling! Earthling!" screamed the empress, trembling with terror on her emerald toilet. "HELP! The palace has been invaded! Guards! Sentry-bots! Protect me! I'm so very, *very* important!"

"Sorry, I didn't mean to. . ." squeaked a panicking Hex, but Glitch tapped him on the head.

"Chik-tic-POP!"

"What? Oh, yeah! Earthling! Right, right. . ." said Hex, remembering how he looked. He glanced back at the hole in the wall. It wouldn't be long before the guards arrived. Hex had to act fast.

"Um, excuse me, Empress, but the thing is. . ." began Hex, trying to think of something earthling-like to say.

"You've destroyed my royal relief zone! And my sentry-bot! Impossible! No one has ever destroyed my sentry-bots before! I thought you earthlings were just weak-minded mud-creatures – I had no idea what you were capable of! Oh, please don't eat me!" pleaded the empress.

"Eat you?" said Hex, feeling queasy at the thought of it, but when he saw the look of fear in the empress's eyes (and her antenna glowing blue with terror), he steadied himself and said, "Yes, eat you! That's what I'll do! We eat anything, us earthlings! Mud, each other . . . and especially space invaders! And I'd know, because I definitely am one!"

"No, please! I'm Her Majestic Green, the Empress Valoona XIII!" squealed the empress. "There's a whole planet of much less significant planetexians out there . . . and I can bring you as many as you can eat! Just spare me!"

"What? No, that's not what I want! I mean, *we* want! We, the earthlings! We want you to call off the invasion of Earth!" said Hex, loudly.

"Call *off* the invasion? For good? But invading's what we *do*. . ." said the empress, not quite able to get her head around the idea, even in the face of being eaten.

"You have to call it off! Look, there are loads of other planets to invade, why not pick one of them?" asked Hex.

"Well, I suppose," replied the empress. "It's just, well, I'd *really* set my sights on Earth. . ."

"Look, you don't seem to get it! You'd better cancel the invasion of Earth and swear never to invade Earth ever again or you're in big trouble!" bellowed Hex, almost starting to enjoy himself. "I mean, look what I did to your sentry-bot! And that was with one sucker – I mean, hand – tied behind my back!"

"I'm sorry!" cried the empress. "Obviously I would *never* have chosen Earth if I thought you were going have a problem with it!"

"Well, I do! I mean, we do! Because there are loads of us, just waiting to attack! A billion! No, a trillion! No, more! What's more than a trillion?"

"Uh, a squillion?" said the empress, clearly not sure.

"Yeah, a squillion!" repeated Hex. "So unless you want a squillion hungry earthlings on your doorstep—"

"No! All right! All right! I'll call off the invasion! Whatever you say!" said the empress.

"Really? That's great! Thanks so much!" said Hex, as he felt Glitch tapping him hard on the top of his head. He turned around to see the empress's guards clambering through the hole in the royal relief zone wall. He looked back at the empress, who was clearly deciding whether to stick to her promise, or shout "Disintegrate the earthling!", but she never got the chance. Hex's tele-belt had started to rumble and fizzle – it had picked up the teleporter signal!

"I have to go now," said Hex. "But don't forget – leave Earth alone, or we'll put Planet X on the menu . . . and you'll be the first course!"

The last thing Hex saw before he teleported was the empress faint and fall off her toilet.

THE HEX EFFECT

Hex re-materialized back inside training zone 78! He immediately checked that he and Glitch were in one piece.

"Did . . . did that just happen? I mean, did we really just do that?" said Hex, not quite able to believe it.

"Chik-klik-POP!" replied Glitch, happily.

"I can't wait to tell. . . Dad!" he said, unclipping his P.A.D. from his belt. "Dad? Are you there?"

HEX! ARE YOU OK, SON? HAS
ANYTHING HAPPENED?

"Hi Dad! Uh, I'll tell you later," said Hex. "Let's just say I think the empress has changed her mind about invading Earth. . ."

YOU DID IT? I KNEW YOU WOULD! YOU SEE? I TOLD YOU TO TRUST IN THE HEX EFFECT! JUST WAIT TILL YOU GET HERE – I HAVE SO MUCH TO TEACH YOU. . .

"But how? How do I get to Earth?" asked Hex.

WELL, THERE MIGHT BE A BLACK HOLE OR TWO TO GET THROUGH . . . BUT NOTHING YOU CAN'T HANDLE! AND DON'T FORGET – I'LL BE RIGHT HERE ON YOUR P.A.D. IF YOU NEED ME BEFORE THEN.

"Actually, there is one thing," said Hex, staring at one of his disguised suckers. "You don't know how to fix a stuck holo-suit zip, do you?"

Hex gave the zip a twist, and it came unstuck. He clambered out of the holo-suit, delighted to be looking himself again. "It worked!" he whooped.

Hex rushed down the corridor and into the vid-zone, where the entire school had gathered to see the empress signal the invasion. He scrambled through the gathered pupils until he found Roswell class, and then shuffled in beside Dooper.

"Hey, Hex – you made it just in time!" said Dooper, his antenna glowing orange with excitement. "Can you believe it? The invasion is actually happening!"

Hex didn't reply. He just took a deep breath and wondered whether the empress would keep her word after all.

"ATTENTION CITIZENS OF PLANET X! HER MAJESTIC GREEN, THE EMPRESS

VALOONA, IS ABOUT TO ADDRESS HER PEOPLE!"

The empress's fat face appeared on the giant holo-screen, and a cheer went up from the whole school.

"Loyal citizens of Planet X," began the empress, sheepishly. "I know how you have all been looking forward to the invasion, which was due to start in less than a minute. However, after much wise, empress-like consideration – and with no outside influences whatsoever – I have decided to *cancel* the invasion of Earth!"

The whole of Sporg's School for Space Invaders seemed to groan in unison! Except Hex, who grinned from hear lobe to hear lobe.

"It has come to my attention that there are much better, more, um . . . invade-able planets out there! Earth isn't good enough to be the next Planet X! I shall pick another planet – a better planet, a planet that will fall before the might of the glorious planetexian army! Tune in for the live final, two weeks from now!"

Another cheer went up from the crowd.

one way or another – he'd done it! He'd ... ... Earth! What's more, ... Hex Effect. Then, through the growing ... from the invasion-hungry pupils, Hex heard a familiar voice.

"So, you managed to get out of the holo-suit, then?"

Hex turned to see Opo smiling back at him.

"Yeah, you just have to twist the zip," replied Hex.

"Do not think for a moment this means your training will stop!" shouted Headmaster Sporg. "There's still plenty to learn, and plenty of planets left to invade! But for now, fill up on gloop – it's lunchtime! Set your tele-belts to 'receive' and prepare to be transported to the ingestion zone!"

As everyone turned their tele-belt dials, Hex turned to Opo. "Can I ask you something?

After you found m... ...e, why didn't you ... was me in the hyper... ...g wrong number. It was...

Opo smiled. "Do you think you're the only planetexian who doesn't want to be a space invader? There are *loads* of us."

"There . . . there are?" asked Hex.

"You'll see," said Opo. "You never know; that luck of yours might be looking up."

"Yeah – maybe it is!" said Hex, as he watched Opo vanish. He turned his tele-belt to "receive" and de-materialized. A second later, he re-materialized in the ingestion zone . . . right in the middle of the Big Gloop Bowl! As the gloop tube opened above his head, he looked up.

"Or maybe not. . ." he sighed.

S l o o o o o o o o o o o o o o o o o r r r r t !

IF YOU LIKE
THIS, TRY THESE
OTHER HILARIOUS
ADVENTURES BY
GUY BASS!

BEING A MONSTER ISN'T
AS EASY AS IT LOOKS!

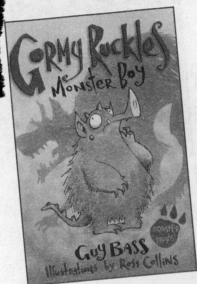